SWEET AS A CUPCAKE

RUCHA PANTOJI

Contents

1. Chapter 1   1
2. Chapter 2   7
3. Chapter 3   14
4. Chapter 4   22
5. Chapter 5   30
6. Chapter 6   36
7. Chapter 7   44
8. Chapter 8   52
9. Chapter 9   61
10. Chapter 10   70
11. Chapter 11   78
12. Chapter 12   84
13. Chapter 13   92
14. Chapter 14   97
15. Chapter 15   104
16. Chapter 16   113
17. Chapter 17   119
18. Chapter 18   125
19. Chapter 19   132
20. Chapter 20   140
21. Chapter 21   147
22. Chapter 22   152
23. Chapter 23   162
24. Chapter 24   168

Contents

25. Chapter 25   175

26. EPILOGUE   183

About Rucha   189

ONE

The notification chimed in the pocket of my apron, sending a wave of pure joy straight to my heart. For the past couple of days, I'd been looking forward to reading those three magical words capable of unleashing butterflies in every girl's tummy and I'm no exception. I wiped my hands with a napkin and unlocked my phone with anticipation rising in my belly. A wide grin stretched across my cheeks as soon as I read those words- *Out for delivery*! I'll finally meet my brand-new oven today. I hope it arrives soon.

Setting my phone aside, I returned to my task. A sweet scent of vanilla and sugar lingered in the air, intertwined with the sizzle of the oil. I gently transferred the golden rings onto the cooling rack and did a little victory dance. For the first attempt, those doughnuts looked quite impressive. I'd be thrilled if they taste as good.

Leaving them to cool, I whisked together melted chocolate chips with fresh cream and a spoonful of honey for the glaze, tempted to try my latest creation.

"Something smells good," Aai perked up, peering into the kitchenette separated by a small wooden frame from the rest of my cute little cake shop.

"Are those doughnuts?" Baba followed with a glint in his eyes. "They look delicious."

I glanced over my shoulder and smiled at my parents. "Yes! Just a moment. I'll bring them out."

They settled behind the counter, giving me an encouraging smile. They have been my loyal taste testers ever since I started baking cakes and cookies about six years ago. They always smiled through my awful attempts and cheered for my best creations. Eventually, I mastered the art.

I love baking. It brings me a sense of comfort and belonging. I still remember that first chocolate cake I sold to my college friend for her sister's birthday four years ago and received so many compliments that I ended up starting a home-baking business, eventually turning it into a cake shop.

Now, nestled in the heart of Rhythm Lane, *Baking Magic* has become my second home.

Luck was in my favor when I decided to open a cake shop. The corner shop among the three at the ground level of my apartment complex was available for rent. Dixit Ajoba, the owner, was more than happy to rent it out to me. I used most of my savings and borrowed some money from Baba to start Baking Magic.

My parents were over the moon. They self-hired themselves to help me out. My father, a retired police officer, took over the deliveries of the orders I receive via my Instagram and the shop's website. Though I've listed my shop on most food delivery apps, my customers often DM me to place a personalized order and Baba, very kindly, delivers them. And Aai helps me keep track of the expenses and finances. She's very thorough with it.

They both adore the shop. They don't bother me or impose their opinions on me. They just want to feel included. With them by my side, Baking Magic is one and a half years old already.

"Do you need any help?" Aai called from the back.

"No, Aai. I'll be out in a minute."

Gently, one by one, I dipped each golden ring into the bowl, enveloping the top of the doughnut with a chocolaty glaze. Sprinkling finely grated chocolate on top, I plated them and quickly snapped some pictures on my phone for Instagram.

Carrying a plate of five doughnuts, I walked out of the kitchenette. "Voila!"

Baba lowered his newspaper and set it aside, curious to try something new. Aai, unable to contain herself any longer, reached for a doughnut, examining it from all angles.

I set the plate down and drummed my fingers on the counter, impatiently waiting for their opinion.

Baba took a large bite, consuming half a doughnut in one go. Aai's rather small bite finished and she took another and then another. I watched them finish the doughnut, testing my patience.

"So?" I eventually asked. "What do you think?"

Baba scratched his beard. "Hm. I'm not sure. Let me try one more."

Aai laughed and swatted his arm, "Don't tease her, Sudhir. It's perfect, Nupur. Try one yourself."

"Baba? Thoughts?"

"As I said," he reached for another doughnut. "I have to try one more. They're amazing."

I extended the plate towards him, taking one myself, and bit into the fluffy deliciousness that melted on my tongue. My chest swelled with pride as I watched my parents devour the rest of the batch. These doughnuts are definitely going on Baking Magic's new menu.

My mind buzzed with plans. Launching new items is just the beginning. Wedding cakes, event cakes, themed desserts – I want Baking Magic to be a part of every celebration. Social media promotions are already running on my channels. I want to try out new recipes for cakes to fill my colorful display case and witness people's joy as they take the dessert home to celebrate special moments. That's the whole reason I love baking. I feel satisfied thinking that somewhere, someone is sharing a bite of the cake I baked with love.

This is the right time. This year ends in a month. Baking Magic will enter the new year with a whole new personality. Freshly painted walls. A larger display case. More functional kitchenette arrangement, and a brand new large oven. I'm so excited. My Pinterest board is full of ideas.

"Do we have any orders to deliver?" Baba asked, wiping his mouth with tissue paper.

"Just one." I took out the pineapple cake from the fridge and packed it in a box, securing the lid with the brand sticker and a ribbon, and sticking a birthday card on top. Placing the box in the paper bag, I gave him the receipt, "Here's the address."

Baba folded and pocketed the receipt and unplugged his phone from the charger. What's with the constant charging, I'd never understand. Whenever his phone battery goes below 60%, he plugs his phone like it's a life-and-death situation. If only he'd lower the brightness and close all the apps he opens throughout the day.

"Okay. I'll deliver it on my way to the market." He grabbed the paper bag and keys to my Scooty. He paused by the door and turned back. "I almost forgot. Some woman called last evening. Ananya Raje. She wants you to call her back. It's about the wedding cake."

"Really?" My heart rejoiced. "Okay, I will."

With a nod, Baba placed the bag of cake in the detachable delivery basket on the back of my Scooty and rode off. Aai went upstairs soon after. "I'm making your favorite potato curry. Don't be late for lunch," she said, before leaving.

I dropped myself on a chair behind the counter and found a Post-it note peeking through my diary with Ananya Raje's number scribbled on it. Drawing a deep breath, I punched her number on the dialer.

As I was about to hit the call button, the bell over the door chimed. Assuming it was my oven delivery, I eagerly stood up. But it was Mr. Dixit, the landlord of my shop, fumbling to push the door with one hand while he tried to steady his walking stick. I rushed to help him and offered him my hand as he carefully took a step forward.

"Hello, Dixit Ajoba," I greeted him warmly, pulling a chair forward. "How are you? Haven't seen you in a while."

"Good good," he replied, groaning as he lowered himself onto the chair. "Knee's acting up again."

Dixit Ajoba and his wife used to stay in an apartment complex on the other side of Rhythm Lane for years until they couldn't climb up the stairs to their flat. Five years ago, they moved to a single-story house a few neighborhoods away. While Dixit Ajji isn't fit enough to visit often, Dixit Ajoba makes frequent trips to Rhythm Lane to meet his friends and never leaves without buying brownies or low-sugar cookies from me, always happy to try something new.

"What would you like to have? Brownies? Cupcakes? Or I also have fresh cookies." I offered him a glass of water. "I was going to call you today to discuss renovation and some changes in the shop interior..." I trailed off when I noticed a tiny crease on his forehead. "But we can discuss that later.

Want some coffee?"

"Nothing today." A mumble escaped his lips. He looked quite out of place. Concern was shadowing his face.

"Everything okay?" I asked. "Do you need more water?"

"No no," he was quick to shake his head.

He drew a deep breath and leaned against the chair. A moment of silence passed, making me nervous. He is usually not this quiet. A tiny wave of anxiety rose from the pit of my stomach. I quickly pushed it back.

He took a small sip of water and cleared his throat, "I'm here to talk to you about something important."

"Sure. What can I do for you?" I kept a smile on my face like I always do.

Dixit Ajoba lowered his eyes, searching for the right words. He cleared his throat before looking back at me. In a very gentle tone lined with worry, he said- "I'm afraid I need to ask you to vacate the shop by the end of December."

The world seemed to shake around me. My vibrant plans for the future, the dreams of expanding the menu and redecorating the shop, all came crashing down.

I could physically feel the color drain from my face. This couldn't be happening. Not now.

TWO

"But we renewed the rental agreement only a few months ago," I tried to control the panic swirling in my belly. "Did something happen? Did I do something wrong?"

"No. Of course, not, Nupur *beti*," Dixit Ajoba exhaled heavily, rubbing his hands on his knees. "We are planning to move closer to the rest of our family. My elder son, you know the one that lives in Nagpur? He has built a bigger house and wants us to move in with him. Grandkids are excited."

I stayed quiet, listening to him. I was happy for Dixit Ajoba and Ajji, but my heart was sinking with every word he said.

"I'm truly sorry for the position this puts you in, Nupur," he continued with a gentler tone. "Wife and I are unable to manage our life alone here. This is just another hassle. And everything happened so fast, I couldn't inform you quicker."

I nodded. "I understand Dixit Ajoba. But..." I could already see the finality of his decision on his face, yet, I tried. "You can trust me. Even if you move, I will keep taking care of the shop and will pay rent on time like always. You don't have to worry."

A sad smile flashed across his face for a moment. Sensing my turmoil, he reached for my hand and gently squeezed it. "I know. And if I were in the position to do that, I'd have happily left the shop with you."

He coughed. I quickly offered him more water.

"I'm sorry Nupur," he gave me a sympathetic look. "I even asked the new owner if he'd let you continue..."

A flicker of hope rose in my heart and vanished as he said, "But he probably plans to start a business of his own. I don't know anything yet."

Tears pooled on the rim of my eyes, threatening to spill over my cheeks. Some of them managed to escape despite my attempt to blink them back.

I can't afford to lose the shop, especially when I have tons of things to do. The uncertainty of what lay ahead weighed heavily on me. A year and a half ago, I was lucky enough to get this shop when the previous tenant relocated his pharmacy shop elsewhere. Dixit Ajoba was so proud to know I was planning to start a cake shop that he immediately let me move in even before we signed the agreement.

Ever since then, I have spent endless hours making the place cozy and magical. It's not just a shop for me. It's my second home. It's a home to *Baking Magic.*

"It's okay Ajoba. I understand," I managed to say. "Let me know if you need anything before you leave for Nagpur. I'll be happy to help."

"I appreciate that, thank you," he said. "I apologize once again for giving you such short notice. It wasn't supposed to happen like this, but life has its ways, you know."

"Yeah," I smiled. "I hope you find comfort around your family, Dixit Ajoba."

He reached for his walking stick resting against the wall and struggled to stand up. I helped him get to his feet and accompanied him until he was settled in a *Rikshaw.*

As I stayed on the pavement outside my shop for a long moment after he left, my mind drifted to the day I opened Baking Magic. How happy I was to have found a perfect place right beneath my flat. Things fell into place shortly after and I never thought, one day, I'll have to restart. I was back to square one, afraid to take the next step.

Back inside the shop, I settled behind the counter, feeling out of place.

Thirty-five days. That's hardly enough time to find a new shop and move my entire setup. Another wave of panic surged through my body. I tried to steady the wobble in my knees.

Oh my god, I'll have to start searching for a new location...Today!

The sudden noise of the phone ringing on the counter made me jump out of my skin. I wiped my eyes, drew a calming breath, and answered the call. "Hi, this is Nupur from Baking Magic."

"Hi Nupur, Ananya this side," came a response.

"Oh, hey Ananya. I was just going to call you. How can I help you?" I tried my best to sound cheerful.

I heard the shuffling of papers on the other side before she spoke again. "I am calling to schedule a meeting with you for a wedding cake. Could you meet me next week?"

"Absolutely. Would you like me to bring some flavor samples?" I asked.

"Yes, that'd be great. I'll text you my address."

"Sure," I replied as we finalized the day and time of the meeting.

I stared at the notes and dates in my diary. My gut twisted into a knot as the realization of how inconvenient it would be to move the shop hit me. I grabbed my phone, flipped the sign to closed, and hurried upstairs.

It's okay! I told myself. Moving into a different shop isn't a big deal. It'll be quick if I start immediately. All I have to do is make a list of shops available for rent in the nearby area, choose one, and move my whole setup before the 30th of December. Seems doable, right?

It'll work out, eventually, I reminded myself as I pushed the door to our apartment and walked inside.

Three plates were already set on the dining table and Baba was serving curry in bowls. Delicious aroma of potato curry danced in the air. My stomach would have rumbled if I had my usual appetite. I wasn't hungry anymore.

"Right on time," Aai smiled, bringing a basket of rotis from the kitchen along with a pot of rice.

I washed my hands and sat across from her. Our beautiful, fun doughnut morning was long forgotten in my mind. I'll have to pause my plans to expand the menu. Redecorating the shop downstairs won't be possible anymore.

I couldn't focus on the meal in front of me, let alone on Aai filling us in with her daily soaps. Baba and I have never watched these shows, yet, we know everything. Truth be told, now we are kind of invested in it. Mostly because Aai makes it sound more dramatic than it actually is.

"One more Roti?" she asked, pausing her story and reaching for the basket.

"No, I'm done." I finished the last bite.

"What? Why?" Her eyebrows knitted at the center of her temple. "Are you not feeling well?" She felt my forehead with the back of her hand. "You don't have a fever."

"I'm okay, Aai. Just not hungry," I replied, half expecting her to serve a roti on my plate anyway. She leaned back and stared at me, scanning my face with concern.

"Do you not like the curry?" she asked. "You always eat extra roti when I make potato curry."

"Aai," I plastered a smile on my face. "I loved the curry. I'm just not hungry today."

"Well then, will you eat some more later? I'll save a bowl for you."

She relaxed the moment I said, "Sure."

My beautiful mother immediately poured some curry into a big bowl, covered it with a lid, and kept it in the fridge. She returned with apple slices and smiled at me when I took one.

As per our daily routine, I helped her wash the dishes and clean the kitchen counter. We often spend those 20 minutes gossiping about someone from our extended family, mostly the nosy and quite annoying aunt of mine, Vinita Kaki. Though my head was buzzing, I tried to participate in the conversation to avoid any further questions from her.

There's no way I'd tell my parents about the shop before I figure it out myself. Causing them any sort of stress is the last thing I want. Baba would jump to his feet to help me out if I asked for it. But I don't want him to.

Opening a shop was my idea. I'm glad my parents love helping me out. It keeps them occupied. Gives them something to look forward to every day. I want them to enjoy their routine without any worries.

"I should get going," I said, rinsing the last plate. Aai wiped her hands on a napkin and felt my forehead again.

"Maybe you should rest for a couple of hours?"

"I'm fine Aai," I pulled her into a bear hug. "I'll see you later."

As I stepped out the door, Chaturvedi Ajji called from the next door. "Nupur beti, could you help me out please?" She was fiddling with the door keys.

I walked up to her door. The keys were stuck in the latch. Ajji anxiously looked at me.

"Don't worry, Ajji." I gripped the handle and pulled the door while twisting the key. Ajji sighed in relief when I managed to get the key out of the latch.

"Thank you," she brushed her fingers on my cheeks, dropping the keys in her cute little crochet bag. "Our old latch was getting stuck, so Vihaan installed this new one. I'm still learning."

"No problem, Ajji. What are you up to?" I asked, holding her hand as we made our way to the elevator.

"Just woke up from my nap. Was bored sitting at home. Thought I'll spend the afternoon in the dairy."

Chaturvedi Ajoba started a dairy downstairs after he retired as a school principal. Ajji helps him whenever she can, and they both enjoy running the shop together.

She never left my hand until I dropped her off at the dairy. Chaturvedi Ajoba waved at me with a cheerful smile. He was sitting behind the counter, listening to retro music on his new Bluetooth radio. I waved back at him.

In a shop sandwiched between the dairy and my cake shop, I saw Rutu through the glass window, hunched over her sewing machine, tracing a delicate thread across the fabric. I walked past her boutique to my shop that soon wouldn't be mine. I stood outside on the pavement, soaking in the comfort of Rhythm Lane. Familiar faces walked by, smiling at me. My eyes drifted to a book café right across the path where Avni was happily attending to book buyers and café customers. The distinct sounds coming from shops from the whole lane lingered around me.

And then it hit me. This is the sound of Rhythm Lane. These are my people. My best friends and my family. I'd terribly miss them when I move my shop. That's why it felt so big of a deal. I hate change. Who doesn't?

Standing there, I felt lost...like a missing piece of a beautiful puzzle.

THREE

My alarm screeched through the silence of the morning. Startled, I jolted upright in my bed, confused and disoriented. Something didn't feel right. My back ached and my neck was stiff. I opened my eyes to find myself slumped against the wall, my head resting on the cold window frame. I tried to rub sleep off my eyes and reached for my phone on the nightstand, squinting at the screen.

6:30 AM

Yawning, I pulled my hair into a messy little bun, tucking loose strands behind my ears. As I attempted to push the blanket away, my laptop tumbled aside on the bed. Next to it lay my diary, a pen nestled between the pages. Flipping it open, I found the list of shops I'd shortlisted the night before.

The events of the previous day came flooding back in.

I had so much to do in so little time.

Dragging myself out of bed, I took a shower and went downstairs. My breath curled into the cold air of the winter morning. I pulled my cardigan tighter around me and emerged onto the pavement outside my shop. Unlocking the door to Baking Magic flooded my heart with so many memories. Decorating this shop for the very first time. Setting shelves and display cases, baking for the first time, and watching people take away sweets with smiles on their faces. It was nerve-wracking yet so much rewarding.

And now, it felt strange to walk into the kitchenette. Like being in a place that doesn't belong to me. Funny how a small piece of information can change the way you feel about things.

I'd cherish my last month in this place, I decided, as I pulled over my apron. My eyes landed on my new oven, which had arrived last evening. I plugged it in and felt that tiny flicker of excitement despite all the chaos in my mind. My regular routine began with baking cakes in my new oven, refilling the display case with pastries, and cupcakes, restocking the cookie boxes on the counter, and re-adjusting the card rack that sits beside the gift shelf. About an hour and a half later, Baking Magic was set to be opened, but not before a quick Chai break.

"Emergency! Meet me for breakfast?" I dropped a text in a WhatsApp group with Rutu and Avni.

"On my way," Rutu replied almost instantly.

"Keeping Chai and Sandwiches ready," Avni's response came a moment later.

Pulling my hoodie over my t-shirt, I headed across the path to *Among The Pages* book café. That cozy place has been standing on the lane for years.

We arrived here on Rhythm Lane when I was twelve. Baba bought this apartment to have a proper family home. While he traveled through multiple police stations in various towns, Aai and I stayed in this apartment so that I wouldn't have to change schools. Baba was eventually promoted and transferred to Kothrud Police Station where he retired.

Avni, with her radiant smile, became my best friend on the very first day, welcoming me into her life with open arms. We have been practically inseparable ever since. She lives right around the corner with her mother, sister-in-law, and her adorable six-year-old niece. After losing her father and brother tragically a few years back, those three women bravely kept their family bookstore afloat. Avni recently converted it into a book café.

Rutu navigated her way through Rhythm Lane with her wild personality about two years ago, searching for a shop to start her boutique. Avni and I spent the whole evening showing her around the lane. Being two years older than us, she quickly became our big sister. She rented the middle shop for her boutique and got a room in a girls' hostel down the lane. *Rutu's Closet* has been stitching and selling trendy fashion ever since. Now, the three of us run our shops side by side on this charming lane.

"Good morning," I greeted Avni as I stepped inside a café that smelled like books, chai, and warmth.

Avni peered at me over her shoulder with a bright smile, her long, curly hair cascading down her back in a French braid. "Morning. Tea's coming right up. Take a seat." She disappeared into the kitchen and returned with a steaming pot of adrak chai and three cups.

Rutu stumbled into the shop and knocked against the chair before steadying herself. Everything about that girl is chaos. "Sorry," she scrunched up her nose and dropped herself on the couch beside me. We kicked off our shoes and tucked our legs underneath us.

"So?" Rutu cut to the chase, taking a sip of chai. "What's the emergency?"

I held the cup of tea in my palms and let the warmth soak into my skin as I narrated the previous afternoon. "Basically," I concluded. "I need to find a new shop ASAP, and I need your help. Plus, I haven't told my parents yet."

Avni nodded understandingly. "Okay. Don't worry we'll help you."

"Whoever bought Dixit Ajoba's shop," Rutu chimed in after a thoughtful pause, "couldn't you just rent it back from them?"

"Dixit Ajoba already asked. He's not sure what the new owner plans to do. I need a reliable solution."

Avni chimed in with a comforting idea that I politely had to decline. "Why not share my cafe for a while, Nupur? At least until you know what the new owner is doing. I have plenty of space in the kitchen, and I wouldn't mind moving around some bookshelves to make room for your display cases. What do you think?"

I reached out and squeezed her hand. "That sounds tempting, but I don't know, Avni. There's too much uncertainty. It's better if I have a proper place of my own."

She squeezed my hand. "No problem. The offer stands if you change your mind. But I agree with you. We need to find you a new place. It'll be messy to keep moving around without a proper setup."

A comfortable silence settled around us as we sipped our chai, the rhythmic clinking of cups against the saucer the only sound. Suddenly, Stevey, Avni's golden retriever, let out a playful bark and bolted towards the door. Harvey, the German Shepherd, Charlie, the Beagle, and Cookie, the Spitz, followed him, jumping with excitement.

Vihaan braced himself and flung open the door.

"Good morning, kiddos," he crouched down to pet these furry bundles of joy. He kissed them. Stevey and Harvey pretty much tackled him down. Avni laughed, holding her phone up to record the video.

As they eventually calmed down, Vihaan straightened his shirt, free from the immense affection, and beamed at us.

"Morning girls." He sat next to Avni and wrapped his arm around her. "Can I get some tea?"

Avni's cheeks visibly turned pink. Ever since they started dating, we've been waiting to plan their wedding. Avni seems happier than ever with him.

"Of course," she replied, heading back to the kitchen.

"Nishant is on the way," he called behind her.

"Okay. Bringing more sandwiches," came her muffled response through the doorway.

Soon enough, the familiar noise of a Thunderbird motorcycle reverberated through the lane and stopped outside the cafe. Moments later, a man walked in, wearing a black jacket over his white T-shirt and beige chinos. He casually ran his fingers through his hair. The corners of his mouth twitched into a perfect smile and my heart flipped. I often wonder how would it feel to be a reason behind that smile.

His eyes met mine for a brief moment before I quickly looked away.

"Hi, Nishant," Avni greeted him with a cup of fresh tea and a sandwich.

"Thanks, Avni." He dropped his backpack to the floor and settled on the armchair next to Vihaan. Those two are colleagues. Apart from working as hybrid employees in a tech company, they're developing some sort of personal finance app. He spends most of his time here in the cafe, working with Vihaan. His younger sister Prachiti became a part of our group before him. She's a gorgeous and a little extra talkative girl who walked into Avni's café with her college friends and changed our lives for good. She brought us the opportunity to showcase our businesses at an event at her college. That was a dream come true for Avni, Rutu, and me.

"What's new?" Vihaan casually asked, reaching for a sandwich. He took a large bite, smiling at Avni. "It's delicious."

She warmly smiled back at him and then, looked at me. "Actually, it's about Nupur's shop."

"What about it?" he asked, facing me.

"Dixit Ajoba is selling the shop," I filled the guys in with the shop situation.

"Oh," Vihaan nodded, thoughtfully. "Don't worry. I'll help you find a new shop in no time. Preferably nearby? So you won't have to move far."

I like Vihaan. Ever since he moved in next door with his grandparents, I found a brother in him that I never had. We often fight like real siblings. He's the best brother one could ask for. And he earned brownie points for making Avni happy, so we're all glad he came into our lives.

To my surprise, Nishant softly chimed in, "I have a few friends who could help. I can call them."

"That'd be really helpful. Thanks," I hardly have anything to worry about with so many people by my side. A huge weight lifted off my shoulder as we chatted away, sipping tea and enjoying our morning before the rush hours began. Rutu even offered to stalk the new owner of my shop so she could scare him away.

"Or," Avni suggested, rolling her eyes. "We could persuade him to rent out his shop to Nupur."

Rutu giggled. "Nah. That's not shady enough."

I burst out laughing. "Think about it Rutu, whoever it is, will be your new neighbor. You better not ruin it."

She groaned. "I already hate them."

Laughing with my friends was all I needed to feel better. I was almost at peace, *almost*, until my phone rang.

"Excuse me." I walked away from the group to answer the call.

Rutu wiggled her eyebrows. "Who is it?" She whistled. "Is that Ankit?"

She and Avni giggled, loud enough for Ankit to hear on the other end.

My eyes drifted to Nishant for a fleeting moment, for reasons I couldn't describe. I wished he hadn't met my gaze. I didn't want him to know. Not that it matters. I quickly looked away and stepped outside through the back door, into the garden of the book café.

"Hi, good morning," I answered the call, already bored and annoyed.

"Morning," Ankit replied, brightly. "What are you doing this evening? I was hoping we could meet for dinner?"

"Um..." I hesitated. I wasn't in a mood to go anywhere. Especially near him. I'm waiting for the day I muster up the energy to tolerate this guy. I'm afraid that day will never come.

"Please?"

If only I had the freedom to say no. "Alright. 8?" I ended up saying.

"Sure," he sounded a little too happy, pretentious even. "I'll book the table. See you soon."

"Yes, see you." I hung up the call and breathed in the scent of flowers in the garden, watching a butterfly flying from one flower to the other. It's been a while since I felt free, especially after Ankit returned to my life. I wish I could go back in time and tell my father how I feel about Ankit. But it's not that simple when people's hearts and relationships are at stake.

With a sigh, I went back inside only to find all eyes on me, sheepishly smiling.

"Why don't you invite him here?" Avni asked. "We want to meet him."

I flopped back on the couch and came up with a lame excuse. "He's always busy so we end up meeting halfway."

"He can take a day off for you, can't he?" Rutu demanded, popping a piece of cucumber that had fallen from her sandwich into her mouth.

"Maybe. But he is in the middle of renovating their restaurant so I'm not sure."

If they sensed hesitation in my tone, they didn't say anything. One of these days, I'm gonna have to tell them why I don't bring Ankit here.

"Oh shit," Rutu abruptly stood up. "I have to deliver a dress this afternoon. Gotta go."

I followed her suit. "I should get going too. Thank you so much again, all of you. For listening and offering to help."

We were already late for our opening hours by the time we left the café. Avni and Rutu pulled me in a hug. "It'll suck without you here," Avni said. I knew they were thinking the same thing as I was. We are a team. Our shops are so close to each other that we basically work together every day.

"I know!" I hugged them back even tighter.

FOUR

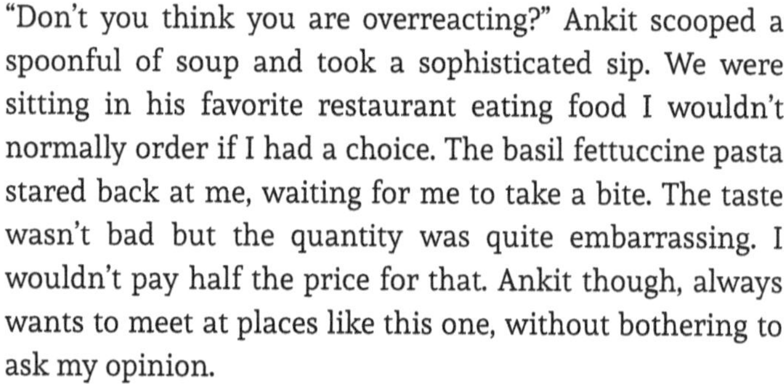

"Don't you think you are overreacting?" Ankit scooped a spoonful of soup and took a sophisticated sip. We were sitting in his favorite restaurant eating food I wouldn't normally order if I had a choice. The basil fettuccine pasta stared back at me, waiting for me to take a bite. The taste wasn't bad but the quantity was quite embarrassing. I wouldn't pay half the price for that. Ankit though, always wants to meet at places like this one, without bothering to ask my opinion.

I was stunned for a second by his question, regretting even mentioning him about the shop. I shouldn't have told him. I shouldn't have agreed to meet him either. And yes, maybe I was overreacting. But I have all the right in the world to feel however I want to feel until I calm down and figure out a way.

"I'm just sharing my thoughts, Ankit. That shop means something to me," I replied, getting annoyed by his expression.

"So what? Shops relocate all the time." He shook his head, "You've always struggled to step out of your comfort zone, Nupur. Ever since you were little."

Ankit and I have been best friends since we were 6 years old. Yet, it feels like I don't even know him. Because now, the man sitting in front of me, speaking weird accent, wearing a ridiculously formal shirt, does not resemble the boy I used to know. His father, Vikram Deo, and my father are college buddies. Even now, after all these years, they hang out like nothing changed. I always admire their friendship that they managed to keep alive. I like to believe Rutu, Avni and I will get old together and hand over the legacy of our friendship to the next generation.

When Ankit and I were little, Vikram Kaka often invited us over to their farmhouse in Mulshi to spend the weekend. Those weekends used to be the most fun days of my life. I loved the peaceful garden, the giant swing in the backyard, the swimming pool, and the delicious food cooked by our mothers. Ankit and I used to fight over who should get the top bunk of the bed, eventually settling on alternate turns.

We were inseparable. I'd bring him a handcrafted gift that he'd keep on the shelf in his room. He'd bring me a flower from the garden and tuck it behind my ear. He was so sweet and caring towards me during our teenage years that I fell for him and he did too. We never really confessed our feelings to each other but it was obvious. We didn't need to say it. We tried to hide it from our parents but our stolen glances and flustered cheeks were hard to miss. Our parents began teasing each other that one day, Ankit and I would get married. Back then, I used to love the idea of marrying him. I liked him and his whole family.

Then we grew up. Ankit went to business school in London out of the blue, and I stayed here. I used to send him messages and stay up late to call him so our time zone could match. But then, his replies became monosyllables and his calls scarce. I'd send a series of messages to him, crying until I had no tears left to shed. He didn't care enough to feel anything. I struggled to believe that Ankit, *my Ankit,* could forget me so easily. Eventually, I took the hint and left him alone, carrying on with my life, hoping he'd realize and make an effort. He didn't, so I moved on. I never told my parents how their beloved Ankit treated me when he was away. They think I'm over the moon to have him back when in reality I'd rather not see him. It took me a long time to suppress my feelings for him, to heal my wounds, to fall out of love.

We weren't even in touch until he returned from London recently and took over his father's restaurant in Koregaon Park. My silly heart did hope that he'd offer some sort of explanation. Who was I kidding? And now, when I don't want anything to do with him, he went ahead and told both our parents he'd like to marry me. Before I got a chance to express how I felt, my engagement was being planned with him and I still haven't told my parents the truth, because I'm scared.

"I tried to convince you to come with me to London to study business," he snapped me back to reality. "You didn't want to step out of your home."

Excuse me?

Now that he is expanding their restaurant and renovating the place, he thinks he is the best businessman to ever exist. If he wasn't Vikram Kaka's son, I would have told him to get lost. But no. Baba wouldn't like it if I became the reason two families parted ways.

"Relax, Ankit," I eventually said, controlling the urge to throw a glass of mojito on his shirt. "I said I'd take care of it. I was just expressing my thoughts. And I'd appreciate it if you don't mention it to anyone, especially our parents."

He heaved a loud sigh. "Yeah don't worry. But I don't understand what the big deal is. I said I can talk to the shop owners near my restaurant, and you'll probably have a shop within a week."

I sipped some water and reached for tissue paper. "I don't want to move that far, Ankit. The rent would be high too."

"See? You don't want to step out of your comfort zone."

I scrunched the tissue paper in my hands, and just to piss him off, took a messy bite of my pasta. I hate sophisticated eating. I like to enjoy my meal on *my* terms.

"Okay. I'll let you know. Tomorrow I am seeing some shops. If I don't find anything in the next 20 days, I'm happy to look at the shops near your restaurant." I plastered a smile on my face.

He nodded. "Now that's my girl."

Oh please. I ain't your girl!

The next 40 minutes dragged so long, I wished the floor could crack open and swallow me whole. Ankit talked about his London life, which is what we talk about... All. The. Time. Whatever we are discussing, he not-so-subtly shifts it towards 'when I was in London'. I wish I could say 'you should go back'.

He showed me some of the pictures on his phone that I'd already seen on his Instagram, but okay. Then he showed me the new renovation work at their restaurant. It's a large, multi-cuisine restaurant and bar. They launched it twelve years ago and have expanded it over the years. Now Ankit does not stop talking about it. *God.*

"Anything else, sir? Ma'am?" The floor manager of the restaurant approached us with a friendly smile.

"Nothing for me," Ankit said. "On a diet," he added, unnecessarily.

I looked at the manager and smiled. "I'll have a brownie please, with Ice cream."

"Coming right up," he replied, conveying the order to one of the waiters.

I shamelessly ate the brownie with ice cream. Actually no, that's not true. I did ask Ankit if he wanted a bite. But he refused and I wasn't going to keep asking. When I was done, I insisted on covering the bill, but Ankit wouldn't listen. So, we settled on splitting it.

"Call me tomorrow night to update me on your shop hunt," he said when we were at the parking lot.

"Sure. I'll call you," I lied. While he went to fetch his car, I walked over to the two-wheeler parking to get my Scooty. We met again by the exit gate. He waved at me from his car and, as a polite gesture, I waved back with a smile.

Wrapping myself in a hoodie and a scarf, and fastening my helmet, I rode back home. It was only 9:45. The city was bustling vibrantly. The weather was quite cold though. I shivered as I drove carefully through the internal roads to avoid traffic.

My phone chimed twice in my purse. Probably Aai, checking in. My parents, bless their hearts, always seem to worry. If I don't respond in another fifteen minutes, calls will start pouring in.

I live with the weirdest roommates ever and I love them.

Aai and Baba were standing on the balcony of our apartment facing Rhythm Lane. I could practically hear my mother's sigh of relief as I arrived in her eyesight.

I parked my Scooty at my usual spot, next to Chaturvedi Ajoba's Minivan, and climbed the flight of stairs to the second floor.

"Why didn't you call when you left?" Aai asked as soon as I entered.

"I forgot, Aai. Not the first time I have come home later than…" I glanced at the wall clock above the television, "…Well, it's only 10:15."

She rolled her eyes.

"Let her be, Mahima," Baba said, smiling at his wife. "How did the dinner go?" he asked me. His enthusiasm always makes me nervous. Our parents are under the impression that Ankit and I are hitting it off. Resuming the friendship we once had. They are hopeful. They are probably designing a wedding card. I don't even want to think about it.

"Fine," I replied, stepping out of my heels and keeping them in a cabinet by the door.

"Just fine?" Baba asked. "What did he say?"

Where do I even begin?

"Nothing new. He showed me pictures of the new décor in their restaurant."

"Yes. They've invited us for dinner."

My eyes snapped towards Baba. "When?"

"Next week," Baba was happy to inform.

"What?" I froze on my way to my room, turned around, and faced my parents. "Did you already say yes?"

"Of course. Why wouldn't I?"

Damn it.

"But I have an important meeting with Ananya next week, Baba. I'll be busy."

"I know," he said. "But your meeting is on Wednesday. The dinner is on Thursday."

There was no point in arguing. If Baba wanted to go, we all must go. Especially when it comes to his best friend. I don't remember a time when Baba declined or rescheduled Vikram Kaka's invitation. He always agrees. Which means, we all agree.

"Okay, Baba," I replied, heading back into my room. I quickly changed into my pajamas and slumped down on my bed, too tired to move. I just wanted to fall asleep and forget about everything just for the night.

"Nupur?" Aai knocked on the door and peeked inside. She pushed the door open and sat down beside me, holding a small bowl of warm hair oil in her hands. "You looked tired. Want some head massage?"

I rested my head on Aai's lap and closed my eyes.

"Everything okay?" she asked and I hated lying to her. But I had to.

"Of course. Just a bit tired. I'd love the massage Aai." I sat on the floor in front of her.

"Oh ho. When was the last time you oiled your hair?" She ran her fingers through my hair. I used to keep my hair short but now my mother won't let me cut them. They've grown a little beyond my shoulders.

"Two weeks ago, if I remember correctly." That earned me a light smack on the back of my head. I chuckled.

Delicately, Aai massaged my head with her softer-than-feather fingers. The refreshing fragrance of Coconut oil soothed me. I kept my eyes closed as she applied oil to my scalp and to the length of my hair, talking about her plan to visit the flea market with Avni's mother, Amrita Kaki.

"What do you want for breakfast tomorrow?" she asked. "How about Upma."

I looked over at her. She bent down to kiss my forehead.

Day after day, I see my parents growing softer and softer. Being their only child, I'm used to having their entire attention on me. Not that they coddled me or anything. The opposite actually. They made sure I grew up to be an independent woman.

And now that I am a grown independent woman, they want me to still be dependent on them. They want me to ask for their help. Demand something. Throw tantrums. With each passing year, they feel I am slipping away from them. They want glimpses of little Nupur now and then to believe

I am still their little girl.

"Can you put green peas in it?"

"You got it," she replied, tying my hair in a braid and securing it with an elastic band.

I turned to look at her. She looked satisfied. Delighted. "Get some sleep," she said.

I smiled. "Good night, Aai."

She planted another kiss on my forehead and left, closing the door behind her.

As night fell over Rhythm Lane, I bundled up in my warm blanket. I desperately wanted to sleep. My eyes were heavy and my body was too tired to move. Yet, my mind was wide awake with a tornado of thoughts making me dizzy.

To distract myself, I binged *Modern Family*, until eventually, I fell asleep.

FIVE

I adjusted the hem of my shirt and slung my tote bag over my arm, heading for Ananya Raje's flat on the ninth floor in an apartment complex in Aundh. The elevator opened to a hallway lined with two flats on each side. Glancing at flat numbers, I walked towards Ananya's door, a knot of anxiety tightening in my stomach.

I wasn't nervous to meet her until I searched for her on social media and found out she was one of the most popular wedding planners in the city. She's been planning lavish events for fifteen years. Always something unique and elegant. She must have a huge list of vendors in her pocket, so I was surprised she picked me, especially for the scale of weddings she plans.

Calming my nerves, I rang the doorbell and stepped back, patiently waiting for the door to open. Ananya, wearing a simple white chikankari salwar suit, greeted me with a warm smile. Black-framed glasses were perched on the bridge of her nose. Her bob hair outlined her oval face. She looked like a woman who'd have answers to all the questions in the world.

"Nupur?" she asked.

"Yes. Hi Ananya," I nervously replied, extending my hand.

She offered a firm handshake with a smile and ushered me in. "Come on in. Make yourself at home." On her way to the open kitchen area, she called over her shoulder. "Sorry, the house is a bit of a mess. Would you like tea or coffee?"

"Um. Coffee sounds good. Thanks."

I sat on the armchair in her living room. Natural sunlight streamed through the floor-to-ceiling glass door to the balcony. Ananya offered me a warm mug of coffee and pushed aside some boxes and papers from the couch to settle down.

The initial meeting went well. She devoured the sample cake pieces and shortlisted two of the designs of four-layered wedding cakes from my catalog. "Radhika will love these," she declared with a confident smile.

I struggled to act cool when I found out that Radhika Thakur, the bride, is none other than the daughter of Nandini Thakur, the founder of the popular classic pearl jewelry brand in Pune. This wedding would be big and I still couldn't understand why was I chosen for this event.

As Ananya and I discussed the rest of the details, a thrilling mix of nerves and anticipation bubbled within me.

"The wedding reception is on the 10th of Jan, 7 PM onwards," Ananya informed. "Will you be able to deliver the cake by 6 PM?"

"Absolutely."

"Great. I'll be in touch," she smiled and gave me her business card. "Here. Just raise an invoice for the advance payment and send it to this email. I'll process it as soon as possible."

I tucked the card in my wallet and stood up to leave. "Um...Ananya, can I ask how did you find me?"

She smiled. "One of my interns found you. She ordered a cake from you a few months ago and loved it. She convinced me to give it a try, so even I ordered a box of pastries. We all loved the taste and quality."

My chest filled with pride. "I'm so glad to hear that."

"Even Radhika liked the pastry sample…so we decided to approach you. I've had some bad experiences with cake vendors and was looking for someone new. I hope this collaboration between us goes well."

A sudden wave of nausea rushed to my throat. I managed to gulp it down. The timing couldn't have been worse. How could I possibly deliver a flawless cake for such a high-profile event in between finding a new shop and relocating?

In the past few days, I've visited about six shops, some of them shortlisted by Vihaan. Even Avni and Rutu accompanied me to view a couple more shops near Ideal Colony. Unfortunately, nothing clicked. Either the rent was too high, or the shop was too small.

I couldn't afford to be picky and I was well aware of that. But Baking Magic cannot be in a shop that barely exists somewhere. I need a proper place where people would want to visit over and over again.

So far, I haven't found a place like that. And it's getting difficult to keep it from my parents.

"You won't be disappointed," I shook her hand and left the premises, feeling excited and terrified at the same time.

Back at the shop, the comfort of my familiar space couldn't quite soothe the growing anxiety within me. I busied myself with baking. Tightening my apron and rolling up my sleeves, I whisked the cake batter until I got the ribbon-like consistency. Layering the baking pan with butter, I poured and evenly spread the batter into the pan and popped it into the oven.

While the cake was baking, I went outside to get some fresh evening air. My wool sweater and cap kept me warm. Rhythm Lane was glowing with streetlights. I sat on the pavement steps, hugging myself.

When I rented out this shop, I always assumed I'd be here for a long time. I never had to search for a shop as this one was available exactly when I needed it, like a sign from the universe. The thought of moving somewhere else never even crossed my mind. And now when the reality has sunk in, I'm finding it difficult to let go.

"Hey." Footsteps followed by a familiar voice neared me. I lifted my eyes to look at the person smiling down at me. "Want some company?" Nishant, with his backpack dangling from his shoulders, stood beside me.

"Oh hey. Sure. Come, sit," I shifted a little to face him. He dropped his backpack and sank next to me.

"Why are you sitting here if you're cold?" he asked when I rubbed my palms together.

I shrugged. "Just wanted some fresh air."

The two of us sat there for a while, under the stars, overlooking a fairly quiet and peaceful lane.

"How's the search for a new shop coming along?" he asked gently.

"Still looking," I replied.

He met my gaze, his smile softening. "I asked around too, but no leads yet."

"That's okay. Thanks for trying though."

He nodded, pressing his lips together in a thin line.

"Anyway," he was kind to change the subject. "Can I get a box of cookies and muffins? Prachiti wanted some and I forgot until now."

"Absolutely. Come on in," I smiled, standing up.

He gathered his bag and followed me inside the shop through the glass door.

As I packed freshly baked cookies in the box, Nishant hovered in the shop, browsing the display case and gift cabinets. He plucked out a small table clock that looks like a vintage telephone from the gift cabinet and curiously admired it. He brushed his fingers over the metal, and a soft smile lingered on his face.

"I got it from an antique shop when Aai, Baba, and I were on a road trip to Lonavala," I told him, securing the box with the brand sticker.

He kept the clock back in the cabinet. "It's interesting."

I grinned. "Thank you. How many muffins?"

"Half a dozen," he said, still browsing the gift cabinet, curiously admiring my collection.

I crouched down to fetch a sheet of unfolded shipping box for the muffins from the bottom drawer, only to realize it was empty.

"Oh," I mumbled.

"Everything okay?" he asked.

"Yes yes," I quickly replied. "I'll be back. Sorry."

"No worries."

I hurried into the kitchenette and stopped in my tracks. The extra box sheets were always on the top shelf, a place I couldn't reach without a chair or Baba's help.

Taking a quick peek at Nishant, who seemed busy typing on his phone, I tiptoed and tried to reach the top shelf. Nope. That has never worked.

Nervously chewing my nails, I looked around. A pair of tongs on the counter caught my attention. I grabbed it, rose to my toes again, and tried to pluck the box. It was hopeless. No, I'm not that short. The cabinet is just too high above the ground.

"May I?" A soft whisper brushed against my skin, sending a shiver down my spine. Nishant stood right behind me. The fragrance of his cologne too familiar. I stood motionless. Scared to fall into him. Gently, I lowered my feet and managed to reply. "Yes, please."

A strong arm with folded sleeves reached over my shoulder, effortlessly retrieving the boxes from the top shelf while my heart pounded in my chest.

"Anything else?" he asked, his voice barely a whisper.

"No, thank you." My cheeks flushed.

He placed the boxes on the counter and stepped back. I took a moment to compose myself, put on my usual smile, and joined him by the display case. "Half a dozen, did you say?"

"Yes," he replied, tapping his fingers on the counter, and chewing the inside of his lips.

I packed his order, my hands still a little shaky. As I handed him the bag, I met his eyes and couldn't help but roll mine. "Oh, come on. You can laugh. I know you want to."

His smile erupted into full-fledged laughter, a warm, infectious sound that filled the shop. Like sunshine breaking through the clouds.

"I'm not laughing at you," he insisted, still smiling.

"Sure you are," I countered, folding my arms over my chest. "That's mean."

"Sorry, I'm just teasing," he chuckled.

He plucked his paper bag from the counter, looked straight into my eyes, and said, "But I'm always here if you need help reaching the top shelf."

And then he left me standing there, breathless and flustered. That's the cutest thing anyone's ever said to me.

SIX

"It all looks grand, Vikram," Baba enthusiastically patted Vikram Kaka's shoulder. "Congratulations."

We were on a tour to explore the newly renovated PunePalette Lounge. Vikram Kaka's restaurant and Bar used to be two stories. Now it has another floor, a rooftop, and an outdoor garden seating as big as indoors with vintage furniture and a gorgeous fountain dancing at the center. People were enjoying their meals with the soft music playing in the background.

"Looks like Nina chose the décor," Aai smiled at Nina Kaki, whose eyes sparkled with pride.

"You know me well, Mahima," she grinned, adjusting the *dupatta* of her silk suit.

Ankit walked beside me, hands in his pockets. Leaning in, he whispered. "She's cute. Thinks she chose it. But the final choice was mine. What do you think? You like it?"

"It's beautiful," I replied with a genuine smile. Everything looked amazing. "Though you can't take credit for the décor. It has Nina Kaki written all over it. This is her taste."

He chuckled and raised his hands in surrender. "Okay. All credit goes to her."

"Good!"

We circled around the restaurant as Nina Kaki proudly showed us the antique pieces she'd found in various exhibitions.

"And…" she turned, smiling ear-to-ear, "Look at this swing. It used to be my grandfather's. My brother recently sent it." A beautiful wooden swing with a gorgeous frame stood on the patio, between two matching armchairs. "Let's take a picture?" she suggested.

My mother, Nina Kaki, and I sat on the swing. "Ankit, click our picture, please," Nina Kaki said, wrapping her arm around me.

"Sure." Ankit held his phone up and snapped a few pictures. "You all look great," he said.

Our fathers were walking ahead as we resumed the tour. Ankit, who was in sync with my pace, fell behind. I looked over my shoulder to find him standing frozen. His phone chimed several times in his hand. His face turned pale. He sneaked a glance at me and quickly silenced his phone.

"All okay?" I asked.

"Yes yes," he gave me an awkward smile. "Just a moment, I'll be there."

"Alright." I caught up with Aai and Nina Kaki. We made our way to an outdoor table reserved for us.

"So, Nupur," Nina Kaki tugged at my arm and made me sit next to her. "How's everything with your shop?"

A pang of worry shot through me. Did Ankit tell her about my shop? I didn't want my parents to find out this way.

I relaxed when she added, "Anything exciting?"

Before I could recover to answer, Aai eagerly chirped, "She received a big wedding cake order from Ananya Raje for Radhika Thakur's wedding."

"Really? That's great, Nupur," Nina Kaki beamed, gently caressing my cheeks.

"Thank you, Kaki."

"We're so proud of our daughter-in-law-to-be, aren't we Vikram?" she grinned.

"Absolutely," Vikram Kaka replied.

I tensed. I'm tired of pretending. Tired of hiding the truth from my parents. I felt nauseated just thinking about how they'd react.

Thankfully, Ankit returned from his long phone call and sank into the chair next to me. The entire conversation took a turn in his favor. My parents asked him all the questions they could think about the renovation and he, the attention-seeker, thoroughly enjoyed answering them. The spotlight never left him throughout the dinner.

The food was amazing. Vikram Kaka ordered three kinds of gravies along with naan, rotis, and pulav made in ghee. Everything was delicious. All of us ate more than we should've, except Ankit. Of course, he had to bring up his diet and the whole segment of conversation around it. I was bored to death. My parents, on the other hand, were charmed by him.

Ankit's parents graciously kept me company, asking me if I was eating enough, if I was enjoying the food, if I needed anything else. But even they were enjoying listening to their son who was away from them for a long time. I didn't mind. I focused on Paneer Tikka Masala.

After dinner, I opened a box of pastries I brought along and served everyone a piece on a saucer.

"Amazing," Vikram Kaka declared, taking another spoonful.

Nina Kaki was next to compliment me. "These are the best pastries I've had in a long time."

"Thank you, Nina Kaki," I beamed with delight. "I'm so glad you enjoyed them. I brought extra for you to take home."

"That's wonderful," Nina Kaki smiled.

I was ready to leave when the dinner was done. But it was only nine o'clock and I knew Baba and Vikram Kaka well enough to predict they'd want to play table tennis. As expected, they made their way to the game room in the restaurant to camp out at the TT table. At least another hour. My patience was running out.

"Ankit, why don't you take Nupur for a walk? Mahima and I will stay here. We have a lot to catch up on," Nina Kaki suggested with a kind of shine in her eyes that made my stomach churn. I knew exactly what they wanted to talk about and I hated the thought of being discussed behind my back about my engagement which I wasn't even interested in.

"Sure," Ankit instantly agreed. He stood up, adjusted his shirt, and offered me a hand.

I pretended I didn't see it and got up on my own. "Where do you want to go?" I asked.

"Nowhere in particular. We'll just walk around the block," he replied, leading the way. I walked alongside him with my arms wrapped around myself. The night air was cooler than I anticipated, and my cardigan wasn't enough to keep me warm. We walked out onto the sidewalk, the soft glow of streetlights casting long shadows across the path.

The question I already knew Ankit would ask as soon as we were out of our parents' earshot landed on me, "So, did you find the shop yet?"

I winced but composed myself. "Still looking."

He tossed away a stone on the path with his shoe. "I talked to a couple of shop owners on your behalf."

I stopped in my tracks, struggling not to snap. "What?"

He smiled, so sure of himself. "It's big enough for you. Not far from here, about a 10-minute drive. And," he continued, turning to walk backward while facing me, "that way, we could spend more time together. Meet every day."

Once again, I regretted telling him about the shop. I don't know what I was thinking when I blurted it out the other day. And now he wants to spend more time? Where was his time when all I needed was a five-minute video call?

I sighed. "Ankit, I appreciate your help, really. But I can't ride for an hour to get there. I need a shop that's within a 4km radius of my home."

"Yes, I thought about that," he continued. "There's a girl's PG just behind those shops in a society. You could move in there for the time being and the shop will be within walking distance. Besides," he added with a foolish grin, "It's only a matter of time until you move in with me."

His eagerness to involve himself in my shop search was smothering me. A sudden need to walk away from him overwhelmed me. No. I couldn't do this. I needed to go home.

With great effort and a steady voice, I managed, "Ankit, if I had an additional budget for my accommodation, wouldn't I just rent a shop nearby without worrying about rent? And," I added, "We're not getting married tomorrow. There's still time."

A flicker of annoyance replaced his smile. "Okay, then what do you want me to do?"

Nothing. I wanted to scream, but I stayed put. "For now, I've got it under control. But I'll give you a call if I need your help."

His sigh was louder than mine. He wanted to convince me further, I could see it on his face. Thankfully, at the right moment, my phone rang. I prayed it would be my father, ready to leave.

But no…it was Dixit Ajoba.

I frowned. Dixit Ajoba never calls at odd hours. A train of thought ran across my mind.

"Are you going to answer that?" Ankit asked, glancing between me and my ringing phone.

"Yes. Excuse me for a moment." I walked away from him.

"Hello? Dixit Ajoba, are you okay?"

"Yes yes, Nupur *beti*. Forgive me for disturbing you, but I wanted to share an idea with you," his voice crackled through the phone.

I relaxed a little. "Sure. I'd love to hear."

"I've been feeling terrible about causing you so much trouble with the shop, and I was wondering how I could help."

I chuckled. "That's really sweet of you, Ajoba. You don't have to…"

He gently cut me off, "I want to. And I might have found a perfect shop for you."

"Really?" I exclaimed. "Where?"

"So, I was curious about that shop next to the girl's hostel on Rhythm Lane."

"The Sawant's shop? What about it?"

"Why don't you go ask Mrs. Sawant if you can rent that shop? It's been sitting there empty for years, ever since they left. And now that she's back…"

Confused, I interrupted him, "Wait a minute. Did you say Girija Kaki is back?"

"Yes, she is," he replied matter-of-factly. "I thought you knew."

"I had no idea."

"She returned a few days ago," Ajoba continued. "I can call her and give her your reference. That shop would be perfect for you. It's spacious and has a lovely storefront."

A flicker of hope filled my heart. That shop truly is gorgeous. I didn't even consider that option because Sawant's house and their shop facing Rhythm Lane have been closed for about eight years if not more. A middle-aged man, probably Girija Kaki's brother, occasionally stops by to keep it tidy. None of us ever saw Girija Kaki, her husband Avdhut, or their daughter Sanika after they left for good all those years ago. We don't even acknowledge that house and the shop anymore. It's a part of the lane that hasn't been talked about for a long time.

"Nupur? Are you there?" Dixit ajoba's voice brought me back to the present.

"Yes, sorry."

"So? Would you go meet her?"

"I'm not sure, Ajoba. I mean, she's been away for years."

"I know, I know," he said. "I just want to help, *beti*. It's the least I could do for you before leaving. Please, just go meet her once and we'll see what she says."

His determination made me smile. "Okay, sure. I'll go see her."

"Tomorrow?"

"Tomorrow," I promised.

"I hope she agrees," he said before hanging up.

I won't lie, the idea was tempting. I'd love to have that shop. It's big. Beautiful. And most importantly, it is on Rhythm Lane. I won't have to move elsewhere.

"Who was that?" Ankit asked, impatiently waiting for me.

"Just a client," I lied to avoid getting into a whole conversation about the shop with him. "Let's go back. My heels are killing me."

He looked down at my heels and back at my face. A smile broke on his face and it annoyed me. "Okay. Let's go."

We spent another hour at the PunePalette Lounge before Ankit called a cab for us. Baba settled on the front seat and turned around to face me. "Isn't he nice?"

"Who?"

"Ankit, of course. He called a cab for us," Baba beamed.

That's all it takes? *I* could've booked the cab.

"He's doing all these amazing things to the restaurant," Baba said, locking his seat belt.

"And he was so nice to us today," Aai added.

In their opinion, he'd be an ideal son-in-law. They wouldn't stop talking about him throughout the ride. I tried to participate in the conversation, but my mind was elsewhere, imagining the possibility of the Sawant's shop becoming a new home to *Baking Magic.*

SEVEN

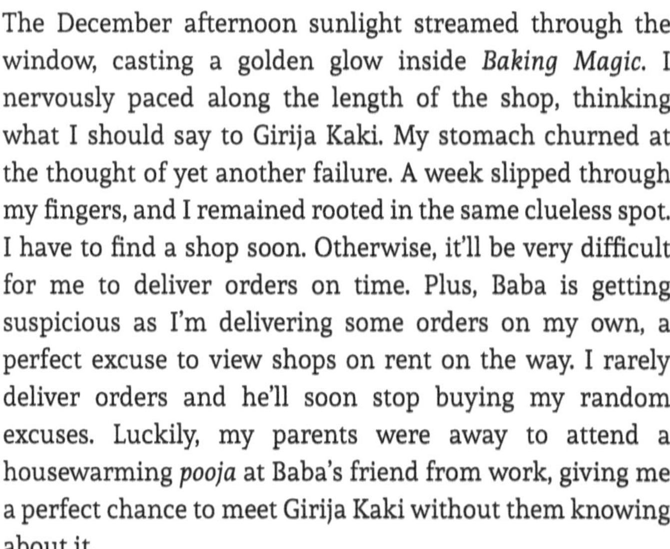

The December afternoon sunlight streamed through the window, casting a golden glow inside *Baking Magic*. I nervously paced along the length of the shop, thinking what I should say to Girija Kaki. My stomach churned at the thought of yet another failure. A week slipped through my fingers, and I remained rooted in the same clueless spot. I have to find a shop soon. Otherwise, it'll be very difficult for me to deliver orders on time. Plus, Baba is getting suspicious as I'm delivering some orders on my own, a perfect excuse to view shops on rent on the way. I rarely deliver orders and he'll soon stop buying my random excuses. Luckily, my parents were away to attend a housewarming *pooja* at Baba's friend from work, giving me a perfect chance to meet Girija Kaki without them knowing about it.

With a pack of freshly baked sugar-free cookies in my hand, I briskly walked along the lane. Warm sunlight wrapped around me, soothing my skin.

As I approached the empty shop, worn-out walls, and rusted shutter door stared back at me. A narrow path next to the shop led to the back where the Sawant residence still stood. A beautiful bungalow with a veranda stretched along the front and the side of the house. Years had passed since I'd last seen Girija Kaki. If I hadn't known she was home,

I'd have thought the house was empty. It was as quiet as ever. No sign of any life within those walls. I hesitated as I stepped over the veranda, a knot of unease tightened in my chest.

I was 14 years old when Girija Sawant, Avdhut Sawant, and their daughter Sanika who was 16 at the time arrived on Rhythm Lane. Girija Kaki was a jolly woman. She always had a soft welcoming smile on her face. Sanika was a spitting image of her. Avni and I befriended her in no time. We'd play together, study together, paint our nails, and braid each other's hair. While Avdhut Kaka worked in a bank, Girija Kaki took care of the house. She'd make and sell ceramic pots and plates. The spare room in their house, connected to the shop, was her art studio. We'd sometimes help her color those ceramic pots and she'd let us keep it. She taught us arts and crafts in the most fun way possible.

The Sawants were here with us like a family and suddenly, three years later, they weren't. We heard rumors about Avdhut Kaka committing fraud at his bank. Nobody knew the whole truth. Avdhut Kaka was arrested a couple of days after the news broke. Soon after that, they all emptied the house and never returned, until now.

Reluctantly, I stepped over to the veranda, knocked on the door, and anxiously waited. The door remained closed. Maybe she wasn't home?

I knocked once again, feeling guilty for bothering her. A minute ticked away without any response from the other side of the door. I was about to turn around and leave when the door cracked open. Girija Kaki peered through the small gap. A shawl was wrapped around her shoulders, over a cream cotton saree. She was only a few years older than my mother but looked so tired and old. Grey strands of hair were tucked in her braid. Her eyes were puffy. My heart twisted at the sight of her.

Her weak 'Yes?' snapped me back to the reality.

"Hello, Girija Kaki. How are you?" I cheerfully greeted her when she opened the door a bit more and stood close to the doorframe. Nostalgia hit me at the sight of her living room after so long. We've played and laughed in her house when life was simpler.

She knitted her eyebrows, confusion shadowing her face.

"I'm Nupur," I wondered if she remembered me at all. "Nupur Acharya? Mahima's daughter?"

She nodded after a long pause but didn't say anything. She didn't even smile and that broke my heart.

I cleared my throat, feeling intimidated by her gaze. "How have you been?"

Her eyes lowered. She looked uncomfortable. Uninterested.

"Fine," she mumbled, clutching the door handle. The Girija Kaki I remember was never so...well, distant. She'd never let a guest stand in the doorway. And she'd smile, at least smile. The lady standing in front of me was nothing like her.

"Um..." I fumbled, trying to come up with an appropriate response. Then I remembered the pack of cookies in my hand. "I brought you some cookies," I said, brightly, extending the box to her. "Welcome back to the neighborhood."

She made no effort to take it from me. I awkwardly lowered the box and smiled. "Have you settled down? Let me know if you need any help."

She gave me an impatient look as if I was wasting her time and invading her space, which I probably was. I wasn't sure anymore if I should be asking her about the shop.

Turned out, I didn't have to.

"Mr. Dixit called me an hour ago," her stare burned my confidence. I briefly considered bolting, but I at least had to try.

"Umm...so, will you rent me your shop?"

As soon as the words left my mouth, she frantically shook her head. "No!" A firm statement. I nearly flinched.

Her grip on the door handle tightened, whitening her knuckles. "The shop is not available for rent. It stays with me."

It wasn't the firmness in her tone that startled me, but the panic in her eyes. Why was she freaking out about it? I wasn't going to steal it from her.

I gulped my embarrassment and fear down before replying. "Oh. Okay. Don't worry, I just wanted to know..."

She kept her gaze hooked to the floor.

"Anyway," I said. "Thanks for your time, Kaki. Have a lovely day. Stop by any time at my shop if you change your mind about cookies."

She closed the door without looking at me and I felt so silly standing there, an uninvited guest. I shouldn't have come. I felt selfish and naive.

With a disappointed sigh, I stepped away from the door. Before coming here, a small part of my heart truly believed I could succeed. It was Girija Kaki, after all. Except, she isn't. Talking to her, even though briefly, felt like talking to a stranger. How sometimes people live so close yet so far away.

A flicker of sadness pinched my heart. Not because I failed to rent a shop but because of the lost charm of that house. The lost person behind that door, all alone.

Leaving Girija Kaki on her own in that empty home felt wrong. What happened to Avdhut Kaka? She must be lonely without her husband and daughter with her. I wondered where Sanika was. What happened in their life after they left?

So many unanswered questions. I felt this sudden tug at my heart. A need to find out more. I was so young when they left I hardly understood what had happened. I vaguely remember Baba meeting Girija Kaki and Avdhut Kaka, hoping he could help with the case in any way, but it was complicated. He couldn't do much for them. Sawant family vanished from Rhythm Lane before anyone knew.

With a heavy heart, I began tracing back the path to my shop. The whole interaction with Girija Kaki was bugging me. The rest of the afternoon, I couldn't get her words, her look, out of my mind as much as I tried to focus on work.

Baking and decorating cupcakes for Avni's book club took my mind off Girija Kaki for a while. I went across to deliver the cupcakes and found Avni, Prachiti, and a few more girls enjoying the early evening breeze in the garden with their books and snacks.

"I was just going to call," Avni gestured at the three-layered snack stand set on the rug. "I've kept the top layer empty for the cupcakes. You can stay if you want," she grinned sheepishly over her shoulder as she went inside the cafe, well aware of my answer. Avni never stops bugging us with her book recommendations. While Rutu and I do enjoy reading occasionally, Avni and her book club girls are crazy. They don't read books, they inhale books and eat stories for breakfast, lunch, and dinner.

"Call me when you're discussing movies," I made a face at her.

Prachiti scooted aside to make space for me. I took off my shoes and sank next to her, arranging the cupcakes on the stand. All the girls sprang to action, taking their phones out to click pictures of the snack stand with their books and posting them on Instagram within moments, tagging @amongthepages and @bakingmagic.

"Hey Nupur Di," Prachiti bumped her shoulder into mine. "Nishant Dada told me about your shop. Let me know if you need any help. I'm also spreading the word so you'll find a new shop quickly."

This girl is so adorable, I pulled her cheeks. "Thank you, Prachiti."

When Avni returned with more snacks and aesthetically arranged them on the stand, I stayed to click a few selfies with them before going back to my shop to attend walk-in customers and pack orders I received from the food delivery apps.

No matter how much I tried to forget my interaction with Girija Kaki, I couldn't get her face out of my mind. An urge to go back there and find out everything about her to try to help her kept bothering me. I distracted myself by editing some baking and icing videos and aesthetic pictures. Applying the usual filter, I posted them on Instagram and Facebook.

Once that was done, I opened my diary and flipped to the page where I had enlisted four more shops. When I called them, the two of them didn't pick up, but the other two told me I could come and see the shop over the weekend. I will have to choose one of them at any cost.

I glanced at the display case and the time on my phone. The case was almost empty as time flicked to 8 PM, so I decided to close the shop early.

I locked the door, pulled the shutter down, and turned on my heels. My face was buried in my phone as I made my way home.

"Ouch!" I bumped into a strong chest and a familiar scent. Two arms held me steady. When I looked up, a pair of brown eyes with a hint of hazel pierced through mine, sending a chill down my spine. I struggled to hold myself upright as one corner of Nishant's lips curled up.

"You okay?" he asked, a smile still lingering on his lips.

"Sorry, I didn't see you."

"That's okay." He ran his hand through his hair. "You heading home?"

"Hm. Closing early tonight."

"Oh okay."

"Did you need anything from the shop? I can open it again," I asked, tucking my hair behind my ears.

"No no. You usually close late, so..."

I nodded. "Just a bit tired today."

A moment of awkward silence later, he shoved his hands in his pocket and said, "I called a few of my friends for your shop. One of them might be able to help. I'll let you know once I hear back from him."

"Really? Awesome. Even I found two more shops. One in Karvenagar and another near CVR college."

"That's great."

"I'm going to go see them this Saturday."

"By yourself?" he asked.

"Um... Yes."

"I could come along," he blurted out, then paused for a moment, and said, "If you want? I'm free this weekend."

"You don't have to spend your weekend viewing shops with me," I replied with a chuckle.

"I don't mind giving you company."

Oh.

I hesitated for a moment. It'd be nice to have some company. But it's Nishant. Though he's a good friend, we have never spent time away from the rest of the group. As much as I'd like to get to know him better, I know for a fact that I'll do something awkwardly embarrassing.

"No pressure," he added.

"I don't mind either," I ended up saying in the spur of the moment. "Only if you are sure."

"I'm sure."

"Okay. Saturday 5 PM?" I asked.

"Works for me."

"Perfect. Thanks a lot."

"No problem."

He smiled and walked away to where his bike was parked outside Avni's café. I stood frozen in my tracks, watching him buckle his helmet. He waved at me before riding away and I went home with my heart thudding louder in my chest.

EIGHT

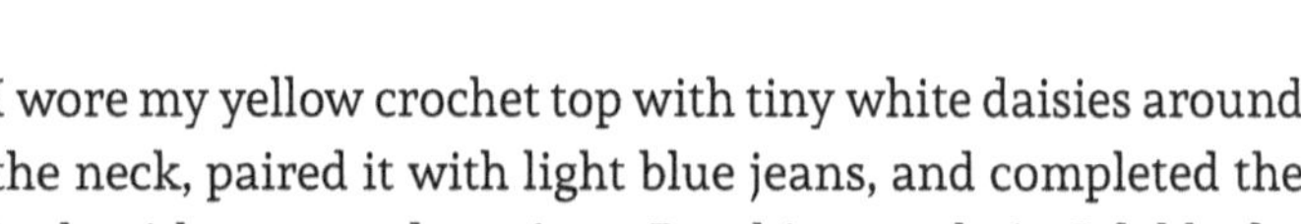

I wore my yellow crochet top with tiny white daisies around the neck, paired it with light blue jeans, and completed the look with cute stud earrings. Brushing my hair, I dabbed a nude shade of lipstick and slung the strap of my sling bag over my shoulder.

"Aai, I'm leaving," I called through the doorway, fumbling to put on my shoes.

Her head peeked out from her room where she was folding her sarees. "Okay. Don't be late."

"I won't."

Baba was out with his friends, so I closed the shop for the evening and told my parents I was going to the market to explore new ingredients. The guilt of hiding so many things from them resurfaced in my mind as I descended the staircase. I always, *always*, tell them everything. Yet, hiding the relocation of my shop and my feelings about Ankit is a necessity until I mustered up the courage to talk to them. I don't know how I'd ever break the news about Ankit. They'll be heartbroken. I'll have to delicately handle it. But I can worry about it later. Finding a shop is my priority.

Tossing a clutter of thoughts away, I stepped outside. The chill of the winter evening whispered around me, carrying a gentle scent of jasmine. I wrapped my scarf over my ears and around my neck as I walked through the gate.

Nishant was perched on his bike, waiting for me. His crisp black shirt hugged his broad shoulders, contrasting perfectly with his blue jeans. He was scrolling through his phone, his hair falling over his forehead. As he checked the rearview mirror to adjust a stray strand, he saw me by the gate and our eyes met. His lips tugged up in a smile so charming, I momentarily froze in my tracks.

Walking up to him felt strange. Good strange. "Hey. Thanks for picking me up." My attempt to sound casual came across a little squawky.

"Anytime!" He gripped the handle of his bike, released the stand with a metallic clang, and smoothly steered it onto the road. "Hop on."

Pushing aside a brief hesitation, I placed my hand on his shoulder as I swung my leg over the back seat. "Comfortable?" he asked as he started the bike.

"Yes." I retreated my hand from his shoulder and immediately regretted the decision.

Nishant navigated the roads of Kothrud, swiftly ripping through the traffic. "So the first shop is in Karve Nagar?" he asked, looking at me over his shoulder as we stopped at the signal.

"Near Karishma Society," I confirmed.

"That's the best lane to have a shop on, don't you think?"

"Absolutely. But this shop is not on the main road. It's a bit tucked away, actually."

He hummed in response and released the clutch as the light turned green. I bumped into his back as the bike jerked forward. My reflexes kicked in and I gripped his shoulder, clutching the fabric of his shirt in my fist.

"Sorry," he said. "You okay?"

"Yeah. I'm fine." This time I kept my hand on his shoulder as he drove. I'd be lying if I said I never dreamt of sitting behind Nishant on his bike, riding through the city with my hand rested on his shoulder. It was as amazing as I imagined it would be. The thought scared me a little. I can't get carried away.

In about 10 minutes, we reached the location. The shop that I had shortlisted was the only closed shop out of the two under a small apartment complex. "Shop available for rent" was written on the closed metallic door with bright red paint.

A man ironing clothes in the dry cleaner shop next door looked over at us. "What are you looking for?"

I gestured at the closed storefront. "We're looking for Mr. Gaikwad, the owner of this shop?"

"Call his number," he suggested. "Haven't seen him today."

I unlocked my phone and dialed the number I already had. He didn't answer. When I tried the number written on the closed door, there was no response either. My heart sank. Did I get the date or time wrong? I quickly checked his message. No, I hadn't. I dialed both numbers again, nervously tapping my foot.

"He's not picking up." Disappointment gripped me from all angles. This shop was ideal, closer, and in a good neighborhood. I glanced at Nishant. "Let's wait for fifteen minutes. If he doesn't come, we'll go to the next shop."

"Sure. Whatever you want," he smiled reassuringly, parking his bike under a tree. "Take a seat while we wait."

I nodded and leaned against his bike, glancing around the neighborhood. He stood next to me. When I met his gaze, he offered, "Don't worry."

My patience ran out within seven minutes. I stared at my phone. Time was running way ahead of my plans. Waiting for Mr. Gaikwad's call was exhausting. Irritation prickled my skin.

"I think we should go," I declared, feeling restless as the clock ticked away. "I don't want to miss out on the other shop. Let's not waste time."

"Alright," Nishant readily agreed, fishing his keys out of his pocket. We started riding towards CVR College.

The shop hunt was proving to be more tiring and complicated than I'd anticipated. Finding the perfect fit for Baking Magic seemed to slip further out of reach with each passing day. At this point, I was desperate for any available shop. I couldn't afford to waste any more time, especially not at the cost of jeopardizing my scheduled orders.

Nishant took a sharp left toward the back of the college nestled among green hills. It's a beautiful neighborhood slightly tucked away from the buzz of the city. I may not get as many walk-in customers but it will have to do.

The view of the blossoming green hills was breathtaking. It gets even prettier during monsoon. Most people come here for a morning walk or a trek to the hills. It's gorgeous. I scanned the surroundings, wondering if *Baking Magic* would fit in here and my heart nodded along.

"That's the one we're viewing today," I pointed at a closed shop sandwiched between a salon and an ATM booth. All three stores looked identical in size and big enough for me.

"Looks good to me," Nishant declared.

I dialed Himanshu's number, the owner's nephew I'd been in contact with. As the phone rang and rang, my hope began to deteriorate. Just as I considered hanging up, Himanshu's voice reached from the other end blended with the background noise of traffic. "Hey Nupur, sorry I'm running late. Stuck in traffic. I'll be there in 20 minutes tops."

I took a deep breath. "Sure. No problem. I'll be here."

"He's coming," I told Nishant, relieved.

"Okay, let's wait for him there," he suggested, pointing towards a bench positioned at the curve of a road leading up to the hills. He parked his bike in an empty spot nearby, and we walked side-by-side. The air was fresh, and a pleasant view of the entire lane stretched before us. One side was lined with shops and the other with a mix of row houses, student hostels, and a basketball court.

I kicked off my shoes and pulled my knees to my chest, hugging them. Nishant shifted on the bench, his hand resting on the back and legs stretched in front of him. "When I was in school," he began, nostalgia laced in his voice. "My friends and I used to cycle here all the way from our neighborhood, just because the path is beautiful. Mostly on early Sunday mornings."

"You'd wake up early on Sundays?" I asked with a teasing smile.

He chuckled. "Yes. I've always been a morning person."

"Really? I was never a morning person until I started my business," I admitted. "Now I have no choice."

"You should join me sometime. We'll cycle up the hill to watch the sunrise and then get breakfast. You'll like it," he said.

"I don't have a bicycle," I replied.

"You can borrow Prachiti's."

I considered it for a moment. I don't remember when I last watched the sunrise through the hills. "You know what? It sounds fun."

"It is," he smiled. I allowed myself to wander into a dreamland for a moment where I was watching a sunrise with Nishant, but quickly returned to reality. No, I don't want confusing feelings. He's a good friend. I can't tangle my emotions and complicate my life.

I glanced at my watch and then at the shop. Himanshu still hadn't arrived. My fingers hovered over his contact on my phone, ready to make another call. Instead, I decided to be patient.

"How are your parents?" I asked, shifting my focus back to Nishant.

His eyes flicked to mine. "Enjoying their retirement life," he chuckled. "Every day is a new adventure for them. They're watching movies together. Going out for dinner at least twice a month. Our garden has never been so beautiful before. And the best of all," he laughed. "They've joined a Zumba class."

I grinned. "Really? That's amazing."

"They're happy," he said, his voice softening. "I'm glad they finally have time for each other."

I smiled at him. "That's true. I'm thinking of sending my parents on holiday for a week or so. Maybe somewhere in the south."

"That's a great idea," he said. "I'll send you some tour packages my parents have explored recently."

"Oh. Okay, sure." I thought talking to Nishant and spending time with him would be awkward. But our conversation flowed easily. We never had an opportunity to get to know each other outside our group of friends. I was surprised to discover he'd been a star cricket player throughout school and college and has a shelf full of trophies.

"You don't play anymore?" I asked, curiously.

"Not as much as I'd like. Sometimes I coach the kids in my neighborhood. They're more than happy to let me tag along."

My mind immediately painted an adorable picture of Nishant coaching cricket to a bunch of kids. A giggle escaped my lips. "That's nice."

As the conversation continued, the sun slowly descended, casting a warm glow across the lane. A gentle breeze rustled the tree leaves above us, sending a few fluttering down to the ground. One landed gently in my hair. Nishant reached to pluck it out. His knuckles brushed my cheeks ever so lightly. A shiver danced down my spine. His gaze lingered on me a moment longer.

"Thanks," I mumbled, still feeling the spark of his touch all the way to my heart.

The distant sound of a car pulling up outside the shop drew our attention. A man in his thirties emerged from the vehicle.

"That must be Himanshu." I stood up, relieved that he didn't ghost me like the previous shop owner.

Himanshu pocketed his phone as he saw us approaching. "Nupur?"

"Yes. Hi, Himanshu."

"Sorry to keep you waiting," he said.

"No worries."

He gestured for us to follow him as he unlocked the shop door and switched on the light, revealing a spacious interior. There was ample space for compact tables and chairs, a perfect spot for the kitchenette in the back, and even a storage area accessible by a pull-down ladder tucked into the ceiling.

"Let me show you." Himanshu pulled the ladder down with a rope attached to it. "Only one person at a time can go up there," he chuckled awkwardly. "Not that it's unsafe. It's quite sturdy. Just narrow."

I peered over at Nishant, he nodded at me to go ahead. So I climbed up the narrow ladder and was surprised to see plenty of space up there. More than what I'd need. I clicked a few pictures for reference and carefully descended the ladder.

"Mind if I take a look?" Nishant asked.

"Not at all. Please." Himanshu held the ladder as Nishant climbed up. We heard a couple of thuds and bangs above our heads. I struggled to hold back a laugh. Nishant crouched a little and came back down, dusting his hands. "You're right. It is quite sturdy."

"So?" Himanshu locked the ladder back up and asked, "What do you think?"

"Can we discuss rent?" I asked, my business mode kicked in.

I was glad I had already done my research when he mentioned the deposit and the rent. "Your quote seems a bit higher than the standard rate in this area, especially for this particular building," I said, my voice firm but polite. "Would you mind if I check with the salon owner next door to get a sense of the rate here?" My face and tone may have shown confidence, but my legs trembled quietly beneath me. I stood tall, unfazed. He must have expected this to happen.

"I'll quickly make a call," he said as he walked outside, away from my earshot.

I looked at Nishant. He raised an eyebrow and smiled. I was grateful for his presence and his patience.

Himanshu returned with a new price quote. I negotiated further and we finally settled on a price that fit my budget. "The shop will be available in the first week of January," he informed me. "I'll call you then to process the deposit and rent."

"I'm open to paying the deposit now," I offered.

"That's not necessary. My uncle will be here to sign the agreement. Probably end of December. You can pay the deposit then."

"Are you sure?"

"Absolutely," he replied.

A sense of relief rose within me. "Excellent. Thanks a lot, Himanshu."

"I'll be in touch," he said.

We shook hands, and after a few more minutes of friendly conversation, he drove away. As soon as his car disappeared from sight, I turned around and jumped in excitement, throwing my arms around Nishant and pulling him into a hug. "Oh my god, Nishant," I squealed, "I can't believe I finally found a shop!"

I stood on my tiptoes to hug him and he slightly crouched down, wrapping his arms around the small of my back. Eyes closed, I leaned into his warm embrace, inhaling the scent of his cologne.

"Congratulations, Nupur. You were amazing." His words whispered through my hair and my eyes snapped wide open.

I quickly released him. "Um. Sorry."

A mixture of amusement and something more, deeper, flashed into his eyes. "Don't worry about it."

Stepping aside, I attempted a casual smile. "Thanks, for being here with me."

"Of course," he straightened his shirt and ran a hand through his hair. His eyes glinted as he smiled and said, "We should celebrate. Let's go."

"Right now?"

"Absolutely. I know a perfect place."

I hesitated.

"Unless you want to go home?" he asked, unable to hide the disappointment in his tone.

"No," I smiled. "Let's go celebrate."

NINE

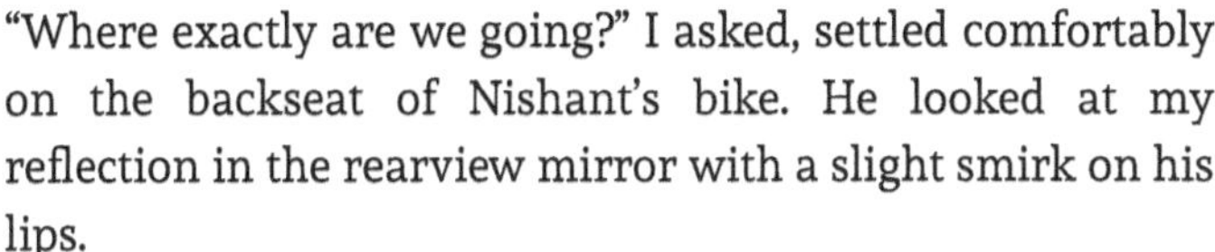

"Where exactly are we going?" I asked, settled comfortably on the backseat of Nishant's bike. He looked at my reflection in the rearview mirror with a slight smirk on his lips.

"Patience."

"Okay." I shrugged, and that earned me a chuckle from him. We rode for a few more minutes before pulling off the main road into a slightly quiet part of Kothrud.

"We'll walk from here," Nishant said, parking his bike in an empty spot along the pathway.

"Sure."

He gestured for me to lead the way into a beautiful alleyway, lined with perfectly manicured trees and illuminated by soft streetlights. It was peaceful compared to the main road not so far from here. I was surprised how much the path ahead was unbothered by the traffic we just left behind.

As we strolled along the path, the warm glow of lanterns and fairy lights hanging by the trees caught my attention. Beneath it, stood a vibrant and lively Chinese food truck. Mismatched tables and chairs were set in front of the truck with a small lantern perched at the center of each table.

My face broke into a wide grin. "I love Chinese street food," I declared.

"I know," he replied, with a gentle smile. "Not difficult to guess when you've mentioned it multiple times. Out loud..." he shook his head, "Not specifically to me."

I couldn't believe he remembered something I hadn't even told him directly. His thoughtfulness overwhelmed me.

"Well, let's not waste any more time." I rubbed my hands together.

Nishant laughed and followed me to the food truck. The tantalizing aroma of stir-fried noodles and exotic spices filled my nostrils. My stomach growled louder.

"Get whatever you want," Nishant said, leaning over my shoulder as I scanned the menu. "We'll share."

Share. I couldn't help but smile. I liked the sound of that. When Ankit and I meet, we never share. Mostly because he orders something I don't like and also because he never offers.

Nishant caught my gaze. "What?" he furrowed his eyebrows.

"Nothing," I shook my head, shifting my attention back to the menu.

Without any hesitation, I placed an order for fried paneer momos, hakka noodles, chilly garlic noodles, Manchurian gravy, and two iced teas.

"What do you want?" I asked, turning to Nishant.

His eyebrows shot up. "Is that all for you?"

"No, of course not," I laughed. "I meant to ask, is that enough for now, or do you want anything more?"

He shook his head. "Let's see how hungry we are after this round."

His teasing was playful, not judgmental. I was just happy I didn't have to think about what to order and didn't have to keep my voice low in a restaurant. I loved everything about the place.

"Nishant, this place is adorable!" I chirped, taking in the colorful decor. "I haven't been here before." We chose the table in a cozy corner near the tree, nestled under the stars and the twinkling fairy lights.

"It's new. Opened about a month ago," he said. My gaze shifted from the fairy lights to him. The glow of the lantern danced in his beautiful eyes and on his face. He looked so handsome, so good. I don't think I've noticed so many things about Nishant before. Like, that adorable zoned-out look in his eyes whenever he adjusts his hair. Or the slight rise of his right eyebrow just before he grins. That enchanting sound of his laughter when he laughs like nobody is watching him.

I wanted to get to know him more.

Resting my elbows on the table and tucking my palms under my chin, I locked eyes with him. "Why don't you tell me a bit about yourself?"

He stopped fiddling with the keys and let out a laugh. "Is this some kind of an interview?"

"No," I giggled. "I just want to get to know you better."

He narrowed his eyes at me, mimicking me by leaning ahead and resting his hands on the table with his fingers interlocked. "What do you want to know?" He held up a finger, "And before you ask, I don't have any favorite color."

"That's not what I was going to ask," I protested and realized I didn't know what I wanted to ask. I wanted to know everything about him. Where to even begin?

I settled on, "What's your secret talent, apart from cycling and cricket?"

"Hmm. Let's see," he rubbed his chin. "I'm pretty good at playing piano."

My jaw dropped. Out of all the things in the world, I didn't expect to hear that. "What? That's amazing."

He smiled. "My Ajoba taught me when I was little. We'd practice every weekend."

"Do you still play?"

"Occasionally," he replied. "I had stopped playing after we lost Ajoba a few years ago. But then Baba requested I play on his birthday and now I have a new ritual with my father."

"I'd love to hear you play something."

"You're always welcome," he replied, and I felt it right at the center of my heart.

"Do you like music?" I asked next, playing with the strap of my bag.

"Yes!"

"What kind of music?"

"Depends on the mood."

"Movies?"

"Again, depends on the mood."

"Do you like watching movies in the theater or at home on OTT?" I asked.

"Anything works. I do prefer certain movies in theater just for the sound effects and visuals."

"I love watching movies in theater," I declared.

"Noted!" he smiled.

"What's your favorite dish?"

"Biryani, if I had to pick one."

"Do you like street food?"

"I wouldn't be sitting here if I didn't."

I grinned.

"Anything else?" he asked, eyes hooked to mine. Lips curled into a soft smile.

"One last question."

"Go ahead."

"What's your favorite color?"

He leaned forward, looked me in the eyes, and answered, "Yellow."

My breath hitched. I looked down at my yellow crochet top as warmth rushed to my cheeks. I tucked a strand of my hair dancing on my face with the wind, behind my ear, struggling to look back at him. When I eventually met his gaze, he asked. "That's all?"

Somehow, I regained control and replied, "For now, yes."

To save Nishant from more questions and me from accidentally embarrassing myself, our food arrived and oh my god, it was a heaven of flavors. Everything was delicious. The perfect mix of spices exploded in my mouth.

We shared each dish and sipped iced tea on a peak winter evening. I was comfortable. The food was good. The man sitting in front of me made me laugh as we ate clumsily. I was happy in that moment. Everything was perfect. I thought I'd wake up from a dream any second now. But that never happened. It was a reality. A truly beautiful one.

"Do you want anything else?" Nishant asked, finishing the last bite.

I wiped my mouth with tissue paper and dropped my back against the chair. "My stomach is going to burst now. I think I ordered a bit much."

"I didn't notice," Nishant teased, smiling.

We paid the bill and remained seated for a while, enjoying the ambiance. "I appreciate you taking time for me today and bringing me here."

He relaxed back in his chair. "Just happy to keep you company. Your negotiation skills are impressive, by the way."

I smiled. "The salon owner next door helped me in a way. I had already spoken to her, and she was more than happy to share what rates I could expect. And I had to get one of the shortlisted shops today," I admitted, feeling a surge of relief. Finally, after a stressful week or so, I could tell my parents about securing a new location for Baking Magic. The thought of Baba's reaction, however, was another concern. He'd be upset, that much was certain, and Aai won't be thrilled either.

The transition wouldn't be seamless. Moving into the new shop will take time and effort. A week, at least, to get everything set up and running again. It meant a temporary closure, but that was a small price to pay. The shop search was finally over.

"Just call me if you ever need any help," Nishant offered as we walked back to his bike. I wished the evening would last forever with us walking down the quiet lanes, talking and laughing.

"I will, thanks," I replied, wondering when will I get a chance to spend such a wonderful time with him again.

A prickling sensation at the back of my mind reminded me to stop dreaming about things that won't come true. Ankit, though far away in his own sanctuary, probably enjoying live music with a fancy drink in his hand, still managed to interrupt my peace. At the end of the day, it was all about him. I longed to confide in my parents, to tell them the truth, that being with Ankit feels suffocating.

It's the exact opposite with Nishant. He's easy to talk to. Safe to be around.

The spiral of thoughts made me nauseated. I wish it wasn't so difficult.

We silently traced back the path, heading towards Rhythm Lane. Though the city was still vibrantly awake, the roads were now fairly calm. As much as I wanted the ride to drag on, we reached the entrance of the lane much sooner than I anticipated.

"Just drop me here. I'll walk the rest of the way," I said. I was craving a walk alone. I needed to clear my head, to process the day.

Nishant slowed down the bike and killed the engine.

"You sure?" he asked, a note of concern in his voice.

"Positive," I offered him a small smile. "Thanks again for the evening. I had a great time."

His face lit up. "Me too."

"See you tomorrow?"

"I'm heading out of town for three days. But I'll see you once I'm back," he replied.

I don't know why that made me sad. Three days aren't much. And it's not like we meet every day. Yet, I felt that unexpected pang in my heart. No. This can't happen. I don't want to feel out of control. I needed the space to process my thoughts, and being around Nishant wasn't exactly helping.

"Oh," I managed, forcing a neutral tone. "Okay, then. Have a good trip. See you when you get back."

"Good night, Nupur," he said as he rode away. I stood there, already feeling his absence deep inside my heart. I turned around and with a steady pace, began walking under the sparkly moonlight shimmering the path ahead.

As I crossed the park and the girls' hostel, I saw Girija Kaki briskly walking down the lane with her arms wrapped around herself. She looked so tired, I thought she'd collapse if I didn't hold her.

"Girija Kaki?"

She winced at the sudden sound and stepped back instinctively, eyes wide staring at me.

"Sorry, I didn't mean to scare you. Are you okay?"

Drawing a deep breath to calm her nerves, she replied in a low voice, "Yes. Just going to get some candles."

I studied her face. She did not look good.

"It's getting late, Kaki," I said, gently. "I can get you those candles."

"That won't be necessary," she lowered her eyes, checked the time on her phone and added. "I'll be fine."

She looked anything but fine. She shivered despite her woolen sweater and the muffler around her neck. Her eyes looked swollen, and if I wasn't mistaken, red even. Something wasn't right.

"Why don't you go home, and I'll bring the candles in 2 minutes?"

I expected her to protest further, to tell me to mind my business. Her silence stretched a moment longer before she agreed. "Thank you," she said.

"I'll be right back," I assured her, watching her walk back towards her house.

The grocery store on the main road was thankfully still open. I grabbed a box of candles and rushed back to Girija Kaki's place.

She was sitting on the veranda, rubbing her shoulders, staring into the void. Her phone was kept face down next to her with the torch on. She looked at me and her shoulders visibly relaxed.

"What's with the power outage, Girija Kaki?" I asked, following her inside the dark house.

"It's been out for hours," she replied, her voice barely a whisper. She fumbled for a matchbox on the dining table, her hands slightly trembling.

I held her hand, "I'll do it, Kaki."

As I lit two candles, their gentle glow illuminated the familiar space. Everything looked the same, yet so different.

That same old wooden sofa and chairs still sat pointing at the television. A blackboard hanging by the wall where we'd play school. Sanika's pictures stood on the TV unit alongside a couple of family pictures. It broke my heart to see their carefree smiling faces now nowhere to be found.

The weight of the questions still hung above me- Where was Sanika? Why was Girija Kaki alone? What happened to Avdhut Kaka?

Girija Kaki coughed, bringing my attention back to her.

"I'll call an electrician for you first thing tomorrow, Kaki," I said, pushing the thought aside for now.

She kept the spare candles in the drawer and sank on the sofa with a huff. She rubbed her back and sipped some water.

"Are you okay, kaki?" I couldn't help but notice her puffy eyes again.

"Yes," she mumbled, leaning behind. "Thanks for the candles."

"Of course," I smiled. "Will you be okay alone tonight? Maybe you could stay with us? Aai would love to have you."

"No, no," she shook her head, her voice weak. "I'll manage."

"Alright, Kaki. No pressure."

"Thank you." She walked me to the door, her steps slow. Emerging out onto the cool veranda, I turned back to her.

"Good night, Kaki," I said, reaching out to touch her arm. Her skin was burning hot. "Kaki! You have a fever!"

She dismissed my concern with a weak wave. "It's nothing. I'll be fine..." she started to say, but her words were cut short. Her eyes fluttered closed as she lost consciousness.

TEN

Panic surged through me as Girija Kaki crumbled to the floor. I wasn't fast enough to catch her. Her eyes remained closed, her breath shallow.

"Kaki? Can you hear me?" I called, my voice shaking with worry.

A low groan escaped her lips as she attempted to stand up. I steadied her with a gentle hand, guiding her back to the couch. I tried offering her water, but her hands trembled too much to hold the glass. "Kaki?" I whispered again.

She weakly hummed.

"Do you have paracetamol?"

She only shook her head.

Resting her on the sofa, I went to her room, frantically searching all the drawers and cabinets for paracetamol but found nothing. I returned with her blanket and wrapped it around her.

"Don't worry Kaki. I'll call someone," I said, fumbling to take my phone out of my sling bag.

With my hand shaking, I somehow dialed Baba's number.

The next hour was a chaotic blur of activities as Aai and Baba brought Doctor Kaka along. He examined Girija Kaki and declared she was dehydrated and the fever was due to weather change, nothing viral.

"She'll be fine in about 2 days," he said, writing down some medication and dietary requirements. He handed over the prescription to me, "Corner pharmacy should be open. She needs these medicines."

Baba took the prescription from me. "I'll get them," he said, already halfway out the door.

"Should she eat anything before the medicine?" Aai asked, her hand resting gently on Girija Kaki's forehead. Girija Kaki's eyes fluttered open for a brief moment to look at her old friend.

"Some turmeric milk," Doctor Kaka suggested. "She may not have appetite."

"I'll make it," I volunteered, disappearing into the kitchen. Thankfully, there was enough milk in the fridge. I set it to simmer with half a teaspoon of turmeric, cinnamon, a couple of cloves, black pepper, and some honey. Pouring the milk into a mug, I hurried outside.

Aai and I guided Girija Kaki to her room. Despite her weakness, she managed to walk with our support.

"I'm okay. I'll be fine," she weakly whispered.

"Girija, you need to rest and let us help you," Aai's firmness got her to relax. With pillows propped behind her, I tucked her in warm blankets.

Baba returned with the medication, which she gulped down with turmeric milk. I was relieved when she finished more than half a mug and closed her eyes.

As she drifted to sleep, Baba approached me, his voice a low murmur.

"What exactly happened?"

I recounted the events, narrating the incident. "I'm glad I saw her. Otherwise, she would have been on her own," I murmured, glancing at Girija Kaki.

Aai rubbed her forehead, "Why is she alone?" she asked the question we've all been thinking about.

"Where's her daughter?" Baba frowned. "Did she say anything to you?"

"No, Baba. I meant to ask about Sanika, but then this happened. And the electricity. I don't know what's the issue…"

He nodded. "I'll check the fuse box. It shouldn't be a big deal."

He went to fix the electricity while Aai and I remained next to Girija Kaki. Deep asleep, Girija Kaki looked at peace. I felt her forehead with the back of my hand. Her fever was better than before.

"You two can go home," I said when Baba returned. "I'll stay with her."

"We'll stay," Aai said. "You might need help."

"I'll be fine, Aai," I assured her. "Go home. I'll call you tomorrow morning."

"You sure?"

"I'm sure."

Reluctantly, my parents left, giving hundreds of instructions. I locked the front door behind them and dragged a comfy armchair into Girija Kaki's room.

Exhaustion eventually claimed me. I wanted to close my eyes for a moment, just to take a small break, but I was terrified to fall asleep in case she needed me. She was all alone. If I hadn't met her, she'd have had no one to look after her. That thought unsettled me. A lot has happened since the evening. I didn't even get a chance to tell my parents about the shop. It was already too late.

With a sigh, I sank further into the armchair and closed my eyes. I wasn't going to fall asleep in that chair, but I couldn't keep my eyes open after a while. At half past three in the morning, I checked up on Girija Kaki and wandered into the living room to lie on the sofa, and fell asleep instantly.

A sudden clattering chime of steel against the tile startled me. I shot upright. My heart hammered inside my ribs, spiking my pulse for a moment before I registered the noise and my surroundings. I hurried into Girija Kaki's room and found her bent over the edge of the bed, trying to pick up the glass of water.

I sprinted towards her. "I'll get it, Kaki." She rested her head against the wall and closed her eyes. I felt her forehead. She wasn't burning anymore.

Rubbing my hands over my face, I looked around to make sense of the time. Early morning light filtered through the curtains.

"How are you feeling?" I asked.

"Better," she replied.

"Good. Do you want anything? Tea? Coffee? Something to eat?"

"I need to freshen up first," she said, attempting to get off her bed.

"Sure." Offering her my arm for support, I helped her to the bathroom. While she brushed her teeth, I made the bed and cleaned up the spilled water.

Drawing the curtains open, I let sunshine pour in, bringing life into the whole room. The fresh scent of the morning, the chirping of birds, and the distant buzz of the new day washed away all the dullness of the night.

Girija Kaki returned to the room, dabbing her face with a napkin. She sat by the window, inhaling the morning air, listening to the distant sound of the city waking up.

A chime of the doorbell echoed into the quiet house. Girija Kaki's brow furrowed in confusion.

"Don't worry, Kaki. I arranged some breakfast for us. I'll be back," I explained, crossing the living room.

Unlocking the door, I swung it open. There stood Avni with a bag of breakfast and Rutu still in her pajamas.

"Thanks for coming on such short notice," I ushered them inside.

"No problem at all," Avni patted my shoulder.

The three of us joined Girija Kaki in her room. Her eyes darted between us as she tried to place the two new people in the room.

"Kaki, this is Avni," I gestured towards her.

"Remember me Kaki? Amrita Joshi's daughter? I brought breakfast for you."

"And this is Rutu."

"Hi Kaki, I'm your neighbor," Rutu pointed at the girl's hostel through the window.

Stunned by so many people conversing with her at once, Girija Kaki remained silent. She stared at us for a moment longer before recovering enough to respond.

"Nice to meet you," she simply said.

While Avni served Poha garnished with coriander on four plates in Girija Kaki's kitchen, I made some tea. Rutu brought Girija Kaki out into the dining area. We all settled around the table.

Girija Kaki ate a spoonful of Poha and smiled at Avni. "It's delicious."

"Have some more, Kaki. I brought plenty."

When we were teenagers, Girija Kaki would make the best Idli Sambar for breakfast. Avni, Sanika, and I would sit around the dining table while Kaki served steaming hot Idlis right from the steamer into our bowls full of Sambar. The morning would carry on with us finishing our homework and joining Kaki in the other room where she'd make ceramic pots and plates. One summer day, she called all the kids from the neighborhood for breakfast and taught us how to make a simple ceramic pot. Later, we all painted it and carried it home.

Those were the days when Girija Kaki was happy.

And now, her gaze kept dropping to her phone. She picked it up, checked the notifications, and kept it back several times.

"Waiting for anyone's call, Kaki?" I asked.

She was quick to shake her head. "No. Just checking time."

Ever since I came here last night, Girija Kaki's phone never rang. Sanika didn't bother sending even a single text, let alone calling her mother.

Sadness in Girija Kaki's eyes was unbearable. I wanted to make her feel seen, heard, and taken care of. Tracking down her daughter was one more thing on my agenda. I'll look into it later.

Rutu, always the chatty one, kept the conversation flowing. We girls filled her in about Rhythm Lane, especially about the Christmas and New Year combined dinner party we were planning to host, the venue for which was still unsure.

"Bigger parties usually happen in the empty yard next to Mrs. Rane's house," Avni said between the spoonfuls.

"You mean here?" Girija Kaki pointed in the direction diagonally opposite her house.

Avni nodded, "Yes. But this year she's not letting us use that space."

"Why?" Girija Kaki asked.

Rutu chuckled. "She hates the noise and doesn't want any mess near her garden. We're still trying to convince her."

Mrs. Rane's house stands at the inner part of Rhythm Lane, right behind Avni's cafe. An empty yard in front of it, which doesn't even belong to Mrs. Rane, has always been a venue for larger events where the entire lane joins in.

Avni took a long sip of tea and added, "The garden of my cafe can be used. We'll see what happens."

"The entire lane will be invited. You must come, Kaki," I said, resting my hand on her arm. "It'll be fun."

To my delight, she nodded.

After breakfast, Girija Kaki took her medicines and decided to take a shower. Avni and Rutu went back to open their shops. I stayed back for another half an hour until two women announced their arrival, bringing more food with them. My mother kept the Parathas in the kitchen and Amrita Kaki filled the cabinet jars with Laddus, Biscuits, and some snacks. Girija Kaki's lunch was sorted and so was her company.

As I went to check on her, I found her dressed in a fresh saree, her hair neatly braided.

"Girija Kaki, I'll be back later today. But you won't be alone. Your friends are waiting for you in the living room if you feel like watching some TV?"

A small smile formed on her lips. "Sure."

She slipped on her woolen sweater over her saree and made her way towards me. She held my hand. "Thank you, Nupur beti."

"Of course, Kaki. And you can call me anytime if you need anything else. Amrita Kaki and Aai will stay with you. You can catch up with them. It's been years since you last met them, so don't mind their extra enthusiasm."

As I accompanied Girija Kaki in the living room, her face lit up a little after seeing her old friends.

"Come, Girija. We'll watch daily soaps," Aai patted a seat next to her on the couch. Three women sat in front of a TV, eager to discuss their favorite shows. Girija Kaki, though not fully comfortable, looked better than before. Maybe this is what she needed- a reminder that she is not alone, that she still has a family.

ELEVEN

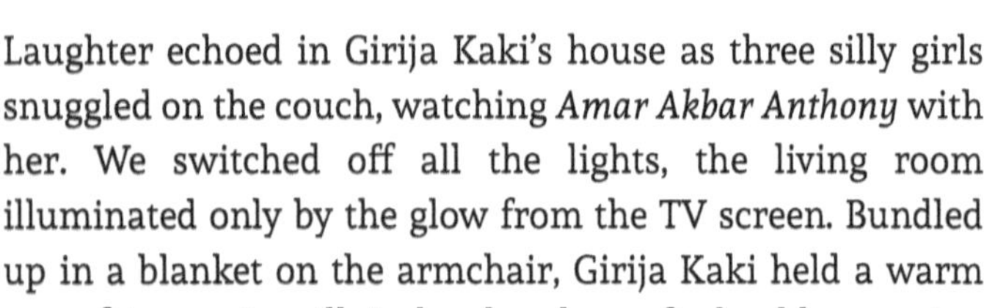

Laughter echoed in Girija Kaki's house as three silly girls snuggled on the couch, watching *Amar Akbar Anthony* with her. We switched off all the lights, the living room illuminated only by the glow from the TV screen. Bundled up in a blanket on the armchair, Girija Kaki held a warm cup of turmeric milk in her hand, a soft chuckle escaping her mouth as the movie rolled. She looked much better than before. Her eyes were no longer puffy and the fever had faded.

For the past two days, someone or the other brought her food and kept her company while I took the night shift. Today, as I was on my way to her home after dinner, Avni and Rutu decided to join in. Rutu found a stack of DVDs of retro movies in the cabinet beneath the television. "Hey look, we could watch a movie," she suggested, browsing the collection.

It took some convincing to get Girija Kaki to join us. But eventually, a smile tugged at her lips and she handed us the TV remote. The old DVD player kept glitching in between, but it was still fun to watch. So there we were, having a girl's night at Girija Kaki's house, probably past her bedtime. She hooked her glasses over the bridge of her nose and rested her head against the armchair.

"Who's your favorite hero, Kaki? Vinod Khanna, Amitabh Bachchan or Rishi Kapoor?" Rutu asked.

Kaki, with a glint in her eyes, replied, "Difficult to pick one. All three are charming." She smiled. "My sister and I used to bunk college and go to the theatre. Back then, we didn't have proper television or these online platforms, so we'd rush to get tickets. We'd stand in a queue for a long time. It was all fun. Now you can just stream it."

I was surprised by how comfortably she was chatting with us. We girls kept her occupied with endless questions and laughed with her. She tapped her fingers against the armchair, synced to the rhythm of the soundtrack. She was clearly enjoying it.

About halfway through the movie, her soft snores filled the room. Girija Kaki, hunched over the back of her armchair, was fast asleep. I considered letting her rest, but she wouldn't be comfortable on that chair. With a gentle tap on her shoulder, I woke her and led her to her room.

"Sorry," she said. "I'm just a bit tired."

"No worries, Kaki. Good night."

"Don't stay up too late," she said, pulling the blankets over her before drifting off to sleep.

After a rather large mug of hot chocolate, none of us could fall asleep. We spread mattresses on the living room floor and continued the rest of the movie in the background.

"Is she asleep?" Avni asked, peering over at Girija Kaki's bedroom.

"Yes."

"She used to be so jolly and vibrant," Avni said, reaching for an extra pillow from the couch and hugging it close. Silvery moonlight cascaded through the window, casting shadows on the other wall. "Did she mention anything about Sanika?"

I shook my head. "No, nothing."

"What exactly happened to them all?" Rutu asked, snuggling into the blanket.

"Her husband was arrested. Something to do with the investment fraud at the bank he was working in," I briefly narrated. "It was hard to believe because Avdhut Kaka was a nice person. They only lived here a few years before he got arrested. Then Girija Kaki and Sanika left out of the blue and that's about it."

"Is he still in jail?" Rutu flipped on her belly to face us.

"No idea," Avni replied. "We don't know the whole truth."

"One thing that I observed in a couple of days," I whispered, ensuring Girija Kaki, if awake, couldn't hear us. "I don't think Girija Kaki and Sanika are talking to each other. Sanika hasn't called her at all."

Sanika's absence in her mother's life was making me so uncomfortable that I spent hours trying to find her on social media. Without her recent picture or location, it was quite difficult to narrow down the search. "I couldn't find her on Instagram," I mumbled.

"We'll try to find her through mutual connections," Avni suggested, stifling a yawn. She closed her eyes, clutching her blanket closer. Rutu was next to fall asleep. I attempted to push my thoughts aside, hoping to get some rest but remained awake until the crack of dawn. The sunrise was still an hour away when sleep finally enveloped me. If Rutu hadn't kicked me in her sleep, I probably would have slept for another half hour. Annoyed, I sat up and pulled her blanket aside.

"Hey! Why'd you do that?" she grumbled, rubbing her eyes sleepily.

"You kicked me," I whined.

"Get your hand off my hair!" Avni cried, pushing my arm aside.

"Oups. Sorry."

She gathered her wild curls into a ponytail, "Do I smell sambar?"

Indeed. The delicious aroma of sambar blended in the air along with the scent of adrak chai. Our heads turned in the direction of the kitchen where Girija Kaki was unloading a tray of Idlis from the cooker. She effortlessly moved in her kitchen, fetching plates and bowls, swirling sambar with a spoon, and pouring tea into cups.

"Breakfast is ready," she announced when she saw us waking up.

"Feeling better, Kaki?" I asked, standing up and folding the blankets while Rutu and Avni rolled the mattresses, clearing the living room floor.

"Much better," she replied with a rather bright smile. "You girls freshen up. I'll set the plates."

It was a beautiful winter morning to wake up to. Birds chirped and the sun shone, bringing pleasant warmth. I spread a rug on the veranda where we all sat in a circle, enjoying Girija Kaki's special Idli Sambar.

"This is delicious, Kaki." Rutu sipped a spoonful of Sambar. "Idli is so soft."

"Have some more." Kaki served us another round.

"Kaki, do you remember you used to make Idli Sambar for us back when we were little? It's as delicious as ever," I said, dipping a piece of Idli in sambar and taking a bite.

Kaki nodded. "You girls were so small back then. I can't believe how grown up you are now."

"Remember when we thought it'd be a brilliant idea to play pretend restaurant with Idli Sambar Kaki made with so much effort?" Avni laughed, almost choking on her food as she recalled a memory.

"Oh my god, yes!" I laughed along. "Sanika dropped the whole pot of sambar. What a mess we created that day."

At the mention of Sanika, all the color from Girija Kaki's face vanished, washing away that rare smile on her face. The laughter froze. Silence hovered over us like a fog.

"You okay, Girija Kaki?" Rutu softly asked.

"Yes yes," she attempted a smile. "I just... never mind. You girls want some chutney?"

I couldn't hold back the questions anymore. I've spent two days with her. I've seen her eyeing her phone, waiting for her daughter to call. I've witnessed her disappointment when her phone never rang. I had to know what was going on.

Anxiously chewing the inside of my lips, I mumbled. "Kaki? Is Sanika okay? Is she coming back anytime soon?"

Girija Kaki's shoulders sagged. She lowered her eyes, trying to hide her ache. I exchanged nervous glances with Avni and Rutu. The guilt of upsetting her mood nauseated me. I regretted mentioning Sanika when I very well knew it was a sensitive topic for her. It took all of us so much time to bring that smile back and I ruined it.

Girija Kaki dabbed her eyes with her pallu. My heart hammered at the possibility of making her cry. I held my breath, ready to apologize again when she calmly replied.

"She's okay. But no, she's not coming back."

"Why?" I blurted out.

"She's busy with work," Girija Kaki shrugged, taking a sip of adrak chai. Avni pinched at my arm, stopping me from asking further questions. The rest of the breakfast was laced with awkward silence as we cleaned our plates and finished our tea.

"Thanks for such a delicious breakfast, Kaki," I managed to say.

She smiled. "Thanks for staying with me and taking care of me. I'm truly grateful."

"Anytime, Kaki," Avni reached for her hand. "Please feel free to drop in at my Book café. We often meet there for a cup of tea. You'll like it."

"Sure," she nodded.

We all left to open our shops. Though I finished all my orders and prepared the inventory for the rest of the day, my mind was elsewhere.

I was determined to find Sanika.

TWELVE

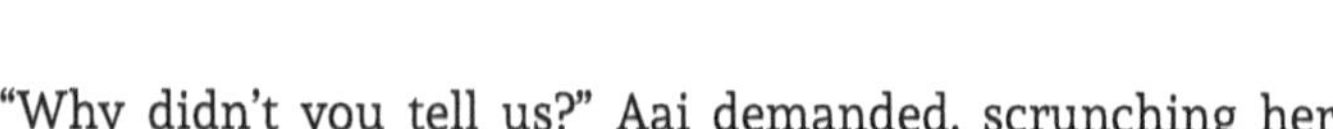

"Why didn't you tell us?" Aai demanded, scrunching her eyebrows. She abandoned the vegetables she was chopping.

Baba slammed shut his book and set it aside. "When did this happen?"

I took a deep breath. "It all happened so suddenly," I explained, trying to sound calm. "Dixit Ajoba is selling the shop, and he doesn't know what the new owner plans to do. I didn't want you to worry, so I found a new place near CVR College."

Baba nodded but stayed quiet. I'd rather him scold me.

"I meant to tell you sooner," I confessed, to break the silence. "But then Girija Kaki wasn't well, and it just…" My voice trailed off.

The entire universe shifted around us as Aai and Baba processed the news, thoroughly scolded me, and eventually calmed down. The frown on their faces took forever to fade. Their reaction, though dramatic, was only natural.

"Here," I offered my phone to Baba. "This is the new shop."

Bracing myself, I rocked back and forth, watching my parents scroll through the pictures of the shop and the neighborhood.

"This looks good," Baba declared, returning my phone. He removed his glasses and sighed, "But you should've told us. We'd have helped."

I smiled to lighten up the mood. "I know, Baba. I just didn't want you to stress unnecessarily. It's all sorted now."

Though Baba's shoulders relaxed after he saw the pictures, I could still see disappointment flash through his eyes. My parents are as attached to the shop downstairs as me. Maybe more. It's their shop too. Their life revolves around it. Not involving them in such a big decision hurt their feelings, wrecking my heart with guilt.

"It'll work out, Baba," I reassured him gently. "It's not that far from here."

He nodded. "You found a good location, Nupur."

He meant it. I could tell that much. But he was hurt nonetheless.

I scooted closer to him and held his hand. "I'll take you for the shop viewing again, whenever you want."

A small smile softened his features. "Sure," he said.

Aai wasn't quite convinced. She declared she'd talk to Dixit Ajoba to reconsider his decision or the new owner to let me rent the shop. She rambled on forever until Baba held her hand. "Mahima, it's okay."

"Aai, don't worry. The difficult part is over. Now we just have to move the shop," I soothed.

"Yeah but..." she frowned. "Nothing can be as good as the shop downstairs, right?"

I couldn't agree more. It's my first shop. *Our* first shop. It holds so much value in our lives that stepping away from it won't be as easy as it sounds.

"We'll make the new shop even better, Aai," I promised, pulling her cheeks. "Here, let me show you some of my ideas."

I showed her some of the themes I had pinned on my Pinterest board. She scrolled through the pictures, nodding her approval. Baba, as expected, called a couple of his friends to inquire about the packers and movers. The tension in the room slowly dissolved. And suddenly, everything seemed easy.

"Okay, I gotta go," I said, plucking a slice of carrot from the chopping board and tossing it in my mouth.

"I'll join you later," Baba informed, resuming reading his book.

"Sure, Baba."

A wave of relief washed over me as I returned to my shop. The afternoon unfolded at a steady pace. I baked cookies and prepared a bunch of pastries. When the time flicked to 5 o'clock, I powered on my laptop by the counter and logged in to answer some pending emails, including one from Ananya. Apparently, the bride wanted some changes in the cake design. She wanted the fondant bridal dupatta to cascade to the bottom layer and the pearls changed from white to gold. Easy enough. I quickly made the necessary changes to the design and sent it to Ananya.

As I was scrolling through the remaining emails, "You look busy," came a voice from the door, making me shudder. I peered over my laptop screen to find Ankit leaning against the door frame, grinning at me.

"I am," I replied, already irritated, wishing I could vanish with a snap of my fingers. Even better if I could make him vanish.

Ankit made his way into the shop and nonchalantly tapped his fingers on the display case. "How about we go for a cup of coffee?"

"I can't," I replied, gesturing to my laptop. "I have work to finish. But I do have coffee here if you'd like some."

"Sure," he said, pouring himself a cup and taking a seat on a chair next to me. When I raised an eyebrow at him, he bit his tongue. "Oh sorry, here." He poured another cup and handed it to me.

I wondered what summoned him here. "So? What brings you here?" I asked.

He chuckled. "Can't I drop in to meet you?"

I narrowed my eyes at him. "You can... but you never do."

He shook his head, still grinning. "Fair enough."

I have all the patience in the world, but Ankit managed to test the limits of my tolerance in seconds. "So?"

He took a long drink of his coffee, then set the cup down on the counter. Wiping his mouth with a napkin, he said, "I have an amazing idea."

"Okay," I dreaded where this was going.

"You know the desserts on our restaurant's menu? We used to order them from a bakery we had a contract with."

"Um-hm...I know." A flicker of suspicion rose in my belly.

"Well, we're putting together an in-house team to bake fresh bread, cakes, cookies, and muffins every day," he explained, his grin widening.

"That's great. Good for you," I replied, not meeting his eyes.

"Exactly! And that's where you come in," he continued, leaning forward. "I'm here to offer you a job. You'd manage a team of bakers, bringing your expertise to our business. We'd work together every day. It would solve your shop issue. You wouldn't even need to find a new location, you'd have a massive kitchen to explore your creativity."

It took every ounce of my self-control not to explode. He doesn't know me at all if he thinks I'll shut my shop forever to work with him.

I kept my calm in check. "That's a wonderful offer..." My voice was surprisingly steady.

"Isn't it?"

"...but I've already found a new shop, and I'm not planning to close Baking Magic."

That stupid grin on his face peeled away. "You found a shop?"

"Yes. Behind CVR College," I replied.

"You never told me!" The disbelief in his tone annoyed me.

Not that I was planning to hide it from him. In fact, I wanted to tell him as soon as possible so he would forget about his idea of me moving into a shop closer to his restaurant. Between the cake orders and Girija Kaki, it completely slipped my mind.

"I meant to tell you," I said with honesty. "It's just been a crazy few days."

He blinked, disappointment clouding his features. For a moment, he looked on the verge of snapping at me. My own anger threatened to resurface, but I sat straighter, composed.

Before he could say anything, his phone began to ring. He pulled it out of his pocket and glanced at the screen. I noticed a sudden change in his demeanor. His face fell and he abruptly stood up. "I have to take this."

He strode out of the shop at once, a little farther than required. I watched him through the window as he spoke frantically into the phone. He shook his head in what looked like panic and ran a hand through his hair. The entire conversation lasted less than three minutes. He returned to the shop with a forced smile plastered on his face.

"Everything okay?" I asked, concern replacing my earlier annoyance.

"Yes yes. Work call," he replied, wiping beads of sweat from his forehead.

He gulped some water from my bottle and typed a text with shaky fingers. Though he claimed he was okay, he looked anything but.

"The offer still stands by the way," he swiftly changed the subject. "Think about it. Especially since it seems like you might have a bit more on your plate than usual." His gaze nervously flickered back to his phone in his hand.

"What's that supposed to mean?" I asked.

He shrugged, avoiding eye contact. "Just... seems like you're juggling a lot right now."

"I manage," I said defensively. "Besides, the new shop is exciting. A fresh start."

"Sure."

I realized he was just mumbling words to keep me distracted. His phone blared again. This time I shamelessly sneaked a peak at the screen before he rejected the call. *Priya.* A girl named Priya was calling him endlessly. This time he silenced his phone.

"Aren't you going to answer it?" I asked, getting restless.

"Not important," he replied. "I should get going."

I glanced at the time on my phone. Ankit wasn't the kind of a guy who'd come all the way here to spend less than half an hour with me. Something was up. He wasn't leaving, he was running away. His body language screamed discomfort.

To his utter displeasure, Baba stepped into the shop when he was about to leave.

"Ankit? Glad to see you here," Baba greeted him with a beaming smile.

Ankit visibly grimaced. He quickly managed to put on a smile. "How are you, Sudhir Kaka?"

"I'm fantastic. I didn't know you were coming."

Neither did I.

Ankit nervously chuckled. "Just wanted to see Nupur."

Baba beamed even wider. "You two can go out for coffee if you'd like. I can stay here."

Alright. Does anyone care whether *I* want to go for a coffee or not?

"Baba, I..."

"We just had a cup of coffee, Kaka," Ankit smiled. "I should get going."

His phone illuminated in his hands again. What is wrong with him? My mind raced. Could Priya be his girlfriend?

Even Baba knitted his eyebrows. "Do you have to answer that?"

"No Kaka, I'll call them back later."

He quickly rejected the call and opened a chatbox to shoot a reply to Priya. A message popped up on his screen and before he could hide his screen from me, I saw the text.

Priya: When are you planning to tell your parents about us?

Our eyes locked. Ankit pocketed his phone but he knew that it was too late. His gaze shifted to my father, who was glancing between me and Ankit with confusion.

"I must go, Sudhir Kaka," he said in a shaky tone.

"Stay for dinner," Baba offered.

"Maybe another time," he managed to reply.

"Oh and," Baba said. "We have a Christmas and New Year's party in the last week of December. You must join us."

Oh god!

"Sure. I'll be there," he said and bolted towards his car. I followed him, trying to match his pace. He was too quick to get inside his car.

"Ankit," I stepped closer to the window. "What's going on?"

"Nothing," he replied.

"Doesn't look like nothing."

He ripped his gaze from the steering wheel to me and pointed a finger at me, flaring with anger. "Look! Mind your business. And, did no one teach you not to look into someone's phone? This doesn't concern you."

Is he out of his mind? It is my concern. He's in my life whether I like it or not. So I have all the right in the world to know what he's doing in his life, especially if it involves another girl's feelings.

"Is she your girlfriend?"

He glared at me with so much anger, I instinctively stepped back. Without answering my question, he just drove away. What on Earth was going on?

Still stunned by his reaction, I turned to get back to my shop and stopped short as I saw Nishant standing by the gate of my building with his backpack dangling from his shoulder. His gaze met mine but he didn't smile.

"Hey. When did you return?" I asked, attempting a casual conversation.

"Last night," he replied. "You okay?"

I smiled. "Yeah. Of course."

He still did not return my smile. He stood there with his hands wrapped over his chest.

"How long have you been standing here?" I eventually gave up and asked.

"Long enough to see him angrily point his finger at you."

THIRTEEN

Midnight uncurled around me as I stared at my laptop screen, attempting to focus on designing a new menu card. My mind kept drifting towards Ankit and Priya. What was going on between them? If she's his girlfriend, why would he still want to marry me? What is he hiding from everyone?

A bitter pang of betrayal shot through me. I still remember the nights I spent sleepless, sobbing into a pillow, over a boy who couldn't care less. Days lost waiting for a call that never came. My best friend, far away from me in a country I only saw through his pictures. I still have our messages, our long conversations slowly fading away until I had nothing left to say. I never deleted those messages. Sometimes, I look at them to remind myself I deserve better. A man who cares for me, loves me. Not a boy so full of himself. And especially not someone who's probably involved in another relationship.

Now that I know there's another girl in the picture, probably as heartbroken as I was, I'm angrier than ever. Though I don't know the whole truth about this Priya, I'm pretty sure whatever is happening between them is going to affect everyone around Ankit.

I leaned against the headrest of my bed and closed the lid of my laptop. There was no point in staring at the screen pretending to work when my mind wasn't calm. Plugging on my earphones, I shuffled my playlist of soft songs and pulled my blanket over my legs. A soft melody played into my earphones as I stared out the window.

Maybe I should talk to Aai first. She'd understand. She can help me confide in Baba later. Time's running out. Emotions are at stake, especially for Nina Kaki who's the most excited among us for this wedding. I wouldn't be surprised if she was already exploring venues. And Aai? Her dream of seeing her daughter in a wedding saree is getting bigger per day. How could I ever back out without breaking the hearts of two mothers?

I could take Avni and Rutu's opinion. There should be an easier way to break the news to my parents. Marrying Ankit is out of the question. I can never risk entering a relationship that I now know for sure won't make me happy. It'll be betraying myself and my parents who want all the happiness in the world for their daughter.

Exhausted, I lay on the bed, staring at the ceiling. I inhaled deeply to stop the buzzing in my head. Nothing worked. It only intensified when my phone hummed under the pillow. Five messages from Ankit. Apologies, justifications, desperate pleas.

Nupur, I'm sorry.

I shouldn't have reacted the way I did.

Priya isn't my girlfriend. She's just an old friend.

You have to believe me.

Call me when you are free, please.

I scrolled through our chat, proof that Ankit hadn't sent me these many messages in a long time. 'Sorry', 'Please', I was surprised Ankit could spell those words. My fingers hovered over the keypad, trying to form a response. But I had nothing to say to him.

Instead, I went to his profile on Instagram and searched Priya. There indeed was a Priya in his list of followers and fortunately, her profile was public.

Her recent picture was a sunkissed selfie from her flat in London with a breathtaking view in the background. The next picture was her sitting on a bench in a park with a flower laced in her hair. She looked beautiful. Ankit is not in any of her pictures, not even the old ones. But I found a couple of picture credits to Ankit, confirming her identity. For a brief, unguarded moment, I considered sending her a message but that'd just make the matter worse.

I flicked back to WhatsApp and tapped on Nishant's message that I had been avoiding since the evening.

Nishant: I need to know if you're really okay because I honestly didn't like the way he talked to you.

He wasn't convinced when I told him everything was okay after he witnessed Ankit's outburst. He wouldn't let me go without knowing if Ankit hurt me. *Not physically,* I wanted to say, instead, I brushed off his worries and earned a concerned stare from him.

I typed a message and deleted it several times before sending- *Hey. Sorry, we didn't get a chance to catch up properly. I'm truly okay.*

I wasn't expecting his reply past midnight. But he read my message and was instantly typing a response.

My heart hitched. I wasn't prepared to answer his questions.

Nishant: No worries. I didn't mean to overhear your and Ankit's conversation earlier.

Me: That's okay. Nothing to worry about.

Nishant: You sure?

Me: Absolutely.

I lied.

Nishant typed for a long moment, probably struggling to put his concerns into words. A short message popped up on my screen- *Okay. Good night, Nupur.*

Good night :) I replied and dropped my phone with a sigh.

I couldn't fall asleep, not with the tornado of thoughts consuming my peace of mind. My bedtime playlist failed to soothe me. So many uncertainties and unanswered questions.

Frustrated, I threw off my blanket, pulled on a hoodie, and went to the sanctuary of my cake shop- the only place immune to the chaotic world outside. Here, amid the blissful silence, nothing could invade my space.

The entire lane was empty, glowing dimly with streetlights. Entering my shop, I locked the door behind me and headed into the kitchenette. A fresh batch of cupcakes would put me at ease, I decided, as I reached for the mixing bowl. The delicate scent of the flavors, the smooth consistency of the batter, and the anticipation of the perfect golden hue of the cupcakes replaced my anxiety with a sense of control. I popped the cupcakes into the oven and waited for them to rise.

When the oven timer ran out, I pulled the tray out and poked a toothpick through them, each time it came out clean. *Perfect!*

While the cupcakes settled to room temperature, I prepared a smooth buttercream frosting.

I hooked my phone to the tripod stand, ready to capture the magic for my online audience. Pressing the record button, one by one, I swirled the frosting on each cupcake with a star piping nozzle to get that floral design and sprinkled some sugar confetti for vibrant colors. Peeling the wrapper away, I sliced the cupcake in two halves and showed the fluffy interior to the camera before I hit pause.

Yes! That's what I'm talking about.

Sitting behind the counter, listening to music, staring into the peaceful quiet of the street, I took a bite of the cupcake, promising myself- I would create my own happiness. I don't know what happens next. But for now, it's just me and my shop.

FOURTEEN

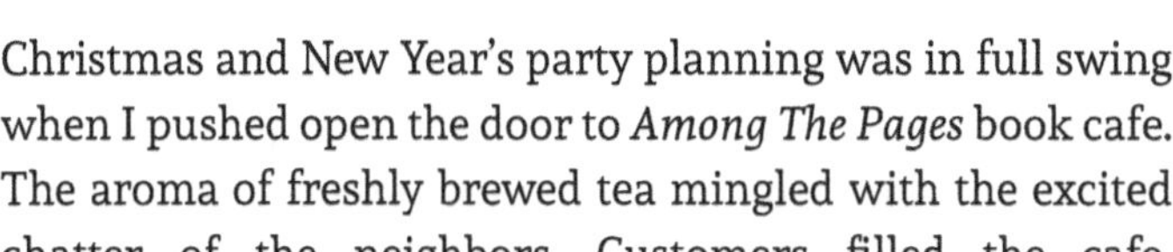

Christmas and New Year's party planning was in full swing when I pushed open the door to *Among The Pages* book cafe. The aroma of freshly brewed tea mingled with the excited chatter of the neighbors. Customers filled the cafe, curiously watching a bunch of us gathered around a table.

Chaturvedi Ajoba was perched on the couch. Everybody else sat on the chairs surrounding him. It looked like he was taking their class. I carried a tray of freshly baked ginger-lime cookies for taste testing and dropped into a chair next to Rutu.

"Nupur," Amrita Kaki, holding a diary and pen on her lap, beamed at me. "Just the person we were waiting for. The cake orders are getting finalized."

"I'm all ears, Kaki."

Amrita Kaki's focus was quickly interrupted by my mother's input on the decoration. Two women discussed the fairy lights and confetti decorations at lengths. Tanvi Vahini chimed in with a suggestion of using artificial flower garlands to outline the benches.

"What's been decided so far?" I whispered to Rutu.

"Nothing at all," Rutu giggled. "Everyone's just been bantering..." she checked her phone. "...for the last twenty minutes."

"Chai is ready!" Avni announced from the kitchen. She brought a large pot of tea and a dozen cups and carefully placed them next to my tray of cookies on the table. Everyone sprang into action, grabbing a cup and a cookie. Vihaan scooted his chair and pulled another next to him to make room for Avni.

"Did Mrs. Rane agree to let us use the yard?" Avni asked, "I wouldn't mind hosting it here, but the space isn't enough."

Right then, Chaturvedi Ajji emerged from the door with a beaming smile. "She agreed."

"Really? How?" My mother was as surprised as everyone else.

"I convinced her it's for the community and she needs to be a little more neighborly," Chaturvedi Ajji replied, taking a seat on the couch next to her husband. She wrapped her pallu around her shoulder and reached for a cup of tea, "Now let's discuss food."

When we were kids, Diwali, Christmas, and New Year parties used to be the previous generation's responsibility. Chaturvedi Ajji and Ajoba have been and will always be active members of the party planning committee. This year they decided, we are old enough to take over, but not without their supervision.

"Avni, make a note," her mother scolded, catching her giggling with Vihaan. "The food order needs to be managed properly. Tanvi and I will help you."

"Yes, ma'am!" Avni struggled to scribble notes as everyone bombarded her with suggestions. Sandwiches, pasta salad, noodles, cutlets, and Rhythm Lane never hosts a party without Pav Bhaji.

"Everybody!" I yelled over the loud chatter. "One person at a time. We're losing track here."

All heads turned towards me. "Latecomers don't get to boss around here," said my mother, narrowing her eyes at me.

Embarrassed, I recoiled, biting my tongue. "Sorry. Please continue."

And like a flick of a switch, the chatter was on within seconds. The conversation was so overwhelming that I rested my head on Rutu's shoulder, trying my best to focus. They hadn't even mentioned the cake order yet, until I finally reminded Amrita Kaki. She passed a piece of paper towards me. "Oh yes sorry, here's a list."

One chocolate cake. A fruit cake. Four dozen muffins of my choice, some with frosting, some without. Two kinds of cookies. Doable.

"What about invitations?" Doctor Kaka asked.

Tanvi Vahini nodded towards the kids, "Looks like they'll be ready in another hour or two."

Back in the day, we kids would spend hours making handmade invitations for the entire Rhythm Lane. Our parents encouraged us to make the cards, mostly to keep us occupied. Now that we are grown, the new generation has taken over the card-making duties. Nidhi sat with other kids, their table overflowing with colored pencils and sketch pens. Older kids were helping younger kids. They were having so much fun, it was adorable.

"Who's arranging chairs?" Chaturvedi Ajoba asked, looking at everyone in a circle.

Vihaan raised his hand with a sigh. "I already volunteered, Ajoba."

"Oh yes. I forgot."

The checklist kept growing. A separate shopping list was getting made by Rutu. I suggested some game ideas that were welcomed and approved with great enthusiasm. Rutu volunteered to prepare a playlist with a mix of old and new songs.

Another round of tea and snacks arrived, keeping the energy levels up amidst the chaos. Avni and Tanvi Vahini somehow managed to juggle party planning with attending to cafe customers and book buyers.

A bell over the café jingled, announcing a new arrival. I gazed back and found Girija Kaki entering the cafe. She momentarily froze in her tracks as a collective hush fell over the table. All eyes turned towards her, surprised to see her. "I'll come later," she turned back.

"No No, Kaki. Please join us." I offered her my chair. She probably felt way out of her comfort zone among so many people, but I wanted her to feel like a part of the family again. She hesitated, her gaze darted nervously around the room.

"Girija, what a pleasant surprise," said my mother with a bright smile.

"Welcome back, Girija. We'd love to hear your creative inputs," Amrita Kaki beamed.

Girija Kaki reluctantly lowered herself into the chair, her eyes scanning the shelves overflowing with books. A small smile touched her lips, "Nice place, Avni beti."

"Thanks, Kaki," Avni smiled back. "Chai?"

Everyone made an extra effort to make Girija Kaki feel comfortable. She was asked to share her thoughts on the decoration and she volunteered to get some flower vases to keep on the tables.

She kept throwing nervous glances at me. I blinked at her reassuringly and stood behind her, placing a hand on her shoulder. Gradually, she relaxed and accepted a cup of tea.

An hour later, the party planning wrapped up. We were all assigned a task leading up to the party held between Christmas and New Year to accommodate everyone's holiday schedules.

"That's all for today," Chaturvedi Ajoba declared. "Thanks for your co-operation."

Vihaan playfully rolled his eyes. "Ajoba. We can manage it just fine, you know? You can rest."

Ajoba ignored his grandson and led the way out, followed by the rest of us. A murmur rose and fell in the café as we poured out one by one. Avni stood by the door, waving goodbye to everyone before sprinting back into the kitchen to manage the evening rush.

"Girija Kaki, would you like me to walk you home?" I asked, offering her my arm.

"Actually," she glanced at my shop. "I was hoping to buy some of those cookies you brought the first time."

"Really? Of course, please come," I rejoiced. Girija Kaki followed me to my cake shop and for the first time, I looked at it through her eyes. Her gaze traveled across the display case, gift shelf, rack of cards, and boxes of cookies. She nodded her approval. "Lovely," she said, brushing her fingers on a tiny metal replica of Shaniwar Wada.

"What kind of cookies do you want? Today I baked some Ginger-lime cookies too."

"Anything works," she answered.

"Okay, then I'll pack you a variety so you can try them all."

While I packed her order, I offered her a seat and served a vanilla muffin with colorful sprinkles on a ceramic plate. "Here you go. I hope you like it."

She carefully unwrapped the cupcake. The delicate design on the plate caught her attention. Her fingers brushed over the pattern and I saw a glint of shine in her eyes. She turned the plate, admiring it from all angles.

"This cupcake is delicious," she said as she took a bite.

"Thanks, Kaki. I'm glad you like it."

"How long have you been doing this?" she asked.

"Started home baking business about four years ago, but the shop itself is only a year and a half old."

She nodded, taking another bite. "And, did you find a new shop?"

I smiled. "I did."

She finished the cupcake, brushing crumbs off her fingers and wiping her mouth with a tissue. Handing the plate back to me, she confessed, "I was rude to you when you came asking for my shop. I'm truly sorry."

"It's okay, Kaki, really," I assured her.

"It's just that, I didn't have a good experience with a previous tenant. And that shop is...well..." her voice trailed off.

"I understand, Kaki. Don't worry about it."

I remember the ugly fight she had had with the previous tenant, a fruit and vegetable seller. She kicked him out a week before the whole family left. Everyone saw the fight and came to their own narratives.

"What was the fight with the previous tenant?" I realized I said it out loud when she shifted in her seat. "Sorry, you don't have to answer that."

"It's okay," a hint of sadness lingered in her voice. "He used to bring his friends in the shop at night. They'd drink alcohol, play loud music sometimes."

"Oh."

"One of them was disrespectful towards Sanika. I couldn't take it anymore. So I threatened to call the police and kicked him out. I'd rather the shop stays closed."

I grimaced. "Gosh. That must've been difficult."

Whispers of the neighborhood gossip resurfaced in my mind. Back when it happened, a lot of people were too quick to judge Girija Kaki, calling her rude and grumpy without knowing the truth. She was simply trying to protect her daughter and maintain peace amidst all the chaos in their life.

"I'm glad you found a new shop," she smiled, lifting the replica of Shaniwar Wada from the shelf. "I'd like to buy this too."

I printed her bill and dropped it into the paper bag. "Here. I hope you like the cookies. Call me if you want more."

She plucked the paper bag from the counter. "Thank you, Nupur. I'll see you later."

"See you, Kaki."

As Girija Kaki stepped outside the shop, I rushed behind her.

"Kaki."

She stopped and turned around. "Yes?"

"Umm. I was wondering...If you ever plan to make ceramic plates again, I'd love to buy a dozen. To serve cakes in my shop."

A long pause stretched between us and I almost expected her to decline my request when she surprised me by saying, "I'll see what I can do." A tiny sparkle of hope shone in her eyes.

FIFTEEN

Fairy lights draped across the branches of the trees twinkled rhythmically. Music and laughter filled the atmosphere with joy. Colorful streamers and flower garlands hanging from the light poles swayed gently in the crisp winter air. The entire community had gathered for the year-end celebration.

Wearing my favorite navy blue knee-length dress with puff sleeves, I arrived at the venue for the fourth time since yesterday. Last evening was so much fun. We'd transformed the empty yard into a party venue. Everyone lent a hand to string the fairy lights to the poles and trees. To Chaturvedi Ajoba's relief, Vihaan brought tables and chairs as promised. Neighborhood children helped us arrange them.

This morning, Avni, Tanvi Vahini, and Amrita Kaki prepared the food while my mother and I baked cakes. With Vihaan and Baba's help, we'd brought everything to the park, before rushing back home to get ready.

Plenty of guests had already gathered, wearing nice clothes. Some refilled their coffee cups while others chose cold drinks. My parents were deeply invested in a conversation with a bunch of neighbors about 'how quickly the year ended'. I couldn't agree more.

Greeting people on my way, I hurried to join Avni standing by a wide table adorned with a lacy red tablecloth.

A delicious buffet was laid out across the table by Avni and Tanvi Vahini with my cakes and cupcakes offering a sweet company.

"Where were you?" Dressed in a gorgeous wavy red skirt and a white top, Avni was grilling sandwiches on a portable toaster.

"Sorry," I bit my tongue, smoothing my dress. "I was shuffling through a couple of options to wear today."

Avni grinned. "I heard Ankit is coming?"

My stomach lurched. A knot tightened in my chest at the thought of facing him. I've been ignoring most of his texts, replying only with an emoji or a simple 'ok'. He still hasn't told me about Priya and I suspect he won't ever explain.

"Don't be nervous," she said, adjusting the pendant on the chain around my neck, "you look stunning."

Rutu, wearing a denim skirt paired with an off-shoulder yellow top sewed by herself, made her way towards us, putting Vihaan in charge of the playlist. Her pink highlighted strand of hair was braided and wrapped over her head like a hairband.

She turned side to side. "How do I look?"

"Beautiful as ever," I replied. "But aren't you cold?"

"A little pain for the love of fashion," she shrugged.

"Love that top," Avni complimented. "I'm gonna borrow it."

"Anytime," Rutu tossed her hair behind and threw her arm over my shoulder. "So?" she said. "We finally get to properly meet Ankit?"

"Guess so." Avoiding eye contact, I pretended to organize cakes that were already organized on the table. I wasn't thrilled about introducing Ankit to my friends. Especially today when all I wanted was to enjoy the party.

"We have tons of questions for him," Avni chirped, buttering the toaster to grill more sandwiches.

"You won't even have to ask. He'll answer them on his own," I said, realizing how sore I sounded.

"Is he chatty?" Rutu asked.

Quite a lot, actually!

"You'll know," I said, already dreading listening to him go on and on about himself.

As I fixed the cupcake arrangement on the stand, my eyes drifted to the entrance. Girija Kaki entered, carrying a box of flower vases. She waved at me for help. "I'll be right back," I excused myself to greet her. "You look lovely, Kaki."

She adjusted the dupatta of her cotton salwar kameez and smiled warmly. "Thank you."

I took the box from her, setting a flower vase on each table. My mother, seated within the circle of ladies, waved at Girija Kaki, pulling her into their conversation. The handmade vases were beautiful. Everyone showered her with compliments.

Leaving them to their endless giggles and chat, I joined my friends back to the food table. We happily served the arriving guests. My fruit cake was a hit, with second servings disappearing almost instantly. Kids kept running past, grabbing cupcakes between their games. My idea of putting up a game zone with a giant Snake-ladder board and Tic-Tac-Toe mat had proven to be kids' favorite corner.

The party continued to fill with a steady stream of neighbors. When we had enough food ready for guests to help themselves with, the three of us wandered into the party with a glass of cold drink in our hands.

"Hey girls," a cheerful voice floated from the entrance as Prachiti walked in. She jogged the rest of the way to us and beamed. "I've brought you gifts."

I glanced past her. My heart fluttered when my eyes landed on Nishant walking in like a rom-com hero. The wind teased his hair. My breath momentarily stumbled upon every step he took towards me.

"Open it," Prachiti eagerly said, giving us a small box wrapped in sparkly pink paper. Inside was a pair of gorgeous handmade silk flower earrings.

"They're beautiful!" I hugged her, taking off my existing earrings and putting on the new one. Avni and Rutu followed suit, making Prachiti happy.

My gaze went back to Nishant. His eyes met mine and the corners of his lips twitched into a perfect smile. Butterflies erupted in my stomach, flying around the two of us.

"Hey, man," Vihaan called out from the DJ booth, drawing Nishant's attention away. With a quick nod, he made his way to his best friend.

"You all look amazing!" Prachiti declared, then turned towards the dance floor at the center. "Come on, let's get this party started before I leave!"

"You're leaving?" I asked, unable to pull my eyes away from Nishant who was now laughing with Vihaan. "But you two just arrived."

"I know," she pressed her lips, "I have a birthday party to catch. A friend of mine is picking me up in fifteen minutes."

"Oh."

"Let's dance!" she said again, practically dragging us to the dance floor.

Vihaan switched the playlist to a Bollywood mashup that had us dancing like nobody was watching. Our synchronized *Thumkas* perfectly complemented the rhythm. Soon, the kids joined us, making us follow their ridiculous jumps. Rutu knew all the hook steps by heart. We copied her as Prachiti recorded a boomerang for us to post on our Instagram story.

"Vihaan!" Avni blared, dancing. "Come join me."

He smirked, looking at her with amusement. Pocketing his phone, he offered his hand and twirled her around the dance floor.

Nishant remained on the sidelines, observing us dance with his hands shoved in his pockets. When I nodded at him, he shook his head.

"Come on, Dada," Prachiti pleaded. "You always do this."

"Do what?"

She rolled her eyes. "I always have to drag you in, and you secretly end up having fun. So ditch the act and join the fun."

He folded his hands over his chest and ignored her. Prachiti, the stubborn little sister, grabbed his hand in her tiny palms and pulled him onto the floor.

He nearly tumbled into me, causing me to lose my balance.

"Sorry." His hand went around my shoulder, holding me steady. My eyes flew to his and I melted into the warmth of his gaze. His eyes scanned mine with a small smile on his face. I found myself falling into them. Lost in the maze of his charm.

"There's my Dada's dramatic entry," Prachiti giggled, snapping both of us out of our trance. I quickly stepped back, hoping nobody noticed my flustered face.

He pulled her cheeks and twirled her. I watched the man roll the sleeves of his shirt over his biceps, run a hand through his hair, and dance to the music so effortlessly, I couldn't tear my gaze away from him. He stepped closer into the circle and began mimicking our moves. His hand brushed mine and I felt that teenage-like spark. We all held hands and circled around kids dancing at the center, giggling. I was having so much fun until...

"Mind if I join?"

A sudden cold voice shattered our beautiful moment. Ankit, with his hand wrapped over his chest, watched us with his judgmental gaze.

"Of course," Avni warmly smiled to welcome him. Everyone stopped dancing at once when they saw Ankit take my hand and pull me a little closer.

"Please carry on," he said to the rest of them with a smile so wide, I cringed.

Avni and Rutu looked at me with smiles on their faces, resuming their dance. When I looked at Nishant, he was back by the DJ booth, his eyes on his phone. As Ankit twirled me, the crowd cheered for us. I hated it. I wanted to tell them the truth. Wanted to scream it so everyone could hear that the man dancing with me was probably playing with hearts. Don't fall for his smile and politeness.

His hand on my waist was burning my skin. I resisted an urge to push him away. Then, to my rescue, the music stopped abruptly. A murmur of the guests rose in the air.

"What happened?" Rutu asked, following Vihaan to the speakers.

"Bluetooth got disconnected."

That small interruption was enough to break the flow. Avni declared she was hungry. Prachiti, giving all of us a quick hug, left with her friend. Kids went back to their gaming zone. And I was awkwardly stuck with Ankit until Baba crossed the lawn to greet him. "Ankit. I'm glad you could make it," he patted Ankit's shoulder.

"Of course, Sudhir Kaka. Great party," he said, glancing around. "We also have a party on New Year's Eve. You guys must come," he smiled at my friends. "All of you are invited.

It's going to be grand."

"We'd love to," Baba replied on everyone's behalf. "You kids get to know each other. We'll catch up later," he said, smiling at Ankit and rejoining the group of men.

The party was supposed to be fun. An escape from tiring work before the new year begins. I was looking forward to it. Ankit's presence pushed all my excitement down the hill.

"So?" Ankit asked, wrapping his arm around my shoulder. "Enjoying the party?"

I was, until you came.

"Yes, absolutely," I replied, forcing a smile. My gaze dropped to his hand on my shoulder.

"Why didn't you tell me earlier? I could've sent my event planners. They'd have taken care of the decoration and food."

"Why? This is good."

"Sure. But these event planners would've helped with the decoration."

My temper flared. My attempt at composing myself seemed to be failing.

"That's not necessary," I managed. "We all worked really hard for this party and everyone seems to be having fun. And," I gestured at the food table. "You'll love the food here. It's delicious."

I freed myself from his grip and followed the rest of the group. We all helped ourselves to the food and grabbed chairs to sit together. Vihaan kept Ankit engaged in a conversation, which to no one's surprise, drifted towards his life in London. Nobody talks about themselves as much as Ankit does.

Ankit rested his hand on my knee, "I wanted to start a restaurant in London." The way he looked at me with so much fake affection made me almost flinch. "If it wasn't for this one, I'd have stayed in London."

Excuse me?

"Aww." Rutu and Avni sang in unison.

Quietly sitting next to Vihaan, Nishant's glare dropped to Ankit's hand on my knee. He gripped his fingers into a fist, knuckles turning white. His eyes met mine just for a second. I held his gaze to reassure him that I was okay, but his discomfort only grew with each passing second.

"If that was true," I said with a fake chuckle, playfully patting his hand and dusting it aside. "You would've talked to me every day."

His eyes darkened for a flicker of a moment. I fiercely held his gaze, knowing well that I was safely surrounded by my people; who noticed my taunt and looked slightly confused.

"More cake?" I asked with a beaming smile.

Four hands shot up, including Nishant's.

"You got it." As I stood up, my phone rang. Himanshu's name flashed on the screen and for some reason, my stomach churned. I wasn't expecting his call until next week.

Desperately hoping everything was ok, I answered, "Hey, Himanshu."

"Sorry to call you at this hour. It's urgent," he said.

"No worries. I can talk."

"So the thing is…"

Each word coming from his mouth pushed the floor beneath me an inch aside until I couldn't stand. My heart sank and my face probably mirrored the disappointment, because my friends were looking at me with concern.

"But I was going to pay the deposit next week, as per your suggestion." My knees wobbled and my voice cracked ever so slightly.

"I know," said Himanshu. "And I'm truly sorry."

"Is there any way you'd reconsider?"

The entire universe shifted around me, throwing all my plans into turmoil. The shop I found with so much effort, the shop I was finally excited about, slipped through my grip. My worst nightmare came true as Himanshu said, "It's not my decision, Nupur. I'd never do that after giving my word. But the shop belongs to my uncle and he has decided to let his friend rent it. I tried my best but I'm helpless."

I didn't realize I was crying until a teardrop fell on my hand and I sank back into the chair.

SIXTEEN

A cloud of uncertainty hung in the air above me. Tears welled up in my eyes, blurring my vision. I tried and failed to gather myself from the dread. Why is everything happening so fast and so not in my favor? That one phone call tore my entire plan into tiny pieces. And in that moment, I felt so tired. So confused.

"What's wrong, Nupur?" Avni's voice floated around me, but I couldn't bring myself to answer. Words dried up in my throat.

I gulped. "I need to go home." My voice came out barely a whisper, at least to my ears ringing with anxiety.

As I stood up to escape home, Aai sensed the tension in the air. She and Baba hurried towards me. Chaturvedi Ajji and Ajoba, and Girija Kaki followed them, confused and worried.

"Nupur?" Aai's panic-struck voice stopped me. "What's happening?" She held my hand and looked me in the eyes. "Why are you crying?" Baba stood next to her and looked so worried, my heart squeezed. I composed myself. Dabbing my eyes, I somehow managed to explain the situation. Words frantically tumbled out of my lips.

Baba remained silent for a moment, his brow furrowed in concentration.

Seeing tears in my eyes, his worried expression softened into a reassuring smile. "We'll find another shop, Nupur. Don't worry."

"But the orders! The wedding cake is due soon. I can't…" More tears overflowed my eyes.

"Hey, relax," Avni said, guiding me back onto a chair. "You can use my kitchen for the wedding cake. Don't you worry about space for a second."

"Yes, but I need to find a new shop quickly."

Baba sat beside me, his gaze steady. "Let's worry about that tomorrow, okay? There's no point in panicking now." He was right. What good would it do?

"I wish I had insisted on signing the agreement that day," I muttered under my breath. I shouldn't have trusted the verbal agreement. That worked with Dixit Ajoba, but not with Himanshu. I should've been careful. I dropped my face into my palms and wiped my tears, ignoring the stains of mascara on my fingers.

In the utter chaos of my lack of planning, Ankit decided to throw more mess onto the pile. I wished he wasn't here. "My offer still stands, Nupur," he said, loud and clear, ensuring everyone, especially Baba, heard him.

I closed my eyes, already tired of facing the conversation he dangerously pulled up. I couldn't muster a response.

"What offer?" Baba asked, his focus shifting to Ankit.

Feeling more energized than before, Ankit leaned forward, "I offered her a job at our restaurant. She can manage the entire baking team. That way, she wouldn't need to worry about her shop."

Then, he uttered something so foolishly offensive that my eyes snapped open in disbelief.

"It's just a small shop anyway. She doesn't have to continue it if she can have an even bigger kitchen and an opportunity to manage a staff."

"Excuse me?" My voice boomed. "Do you even realize what you're saying?"

Of course, he didn't.

He shrugged as if it wasn't a big deal. "I'm just saying, why bother finding a shop when you don't have to continue this small business? You can join our restaurant."

Rage bubbled within me. I felt dizzy and restless. My skin prickled.

I took a calming breath and achieved a steady voice despite the tremble lacing my words. "It might be small, Ankit, but it's *my* business. And I will never give up on it."

"Yes, but it only makes sense..."

Before Ankit could finish, Baba cut him off, pinching the bridge of his nose. "With all due respect, Ankit *beta*," he met Ankit's eyes fiercely. Ankit leaned back, visibly stunned by my father's tone. "My daughter will not accept your offer. She will not close her shop."

"Sudhir Kaka, I'm only saying she doesn't have to get a new shop when I'm offering a better solution."

"I understand what you're trying to do," Baba interrupted with a firm tone. "But she doesn't need a job. She has her own business, which by the way, is doing really well. We've raised her to be independent, and she's more than capable of making her own decisions."

Ankit's face flushed a deep red. It was the first time I'd ever seen him flustered. He probably heard someone disagree with him for the first time in his life. Yet, he did not stop talking.

"You're not thinking it through, Sudhir Kaka." Ankit's eyes darkened. The conversation took such an unexpected turn in front of everyone, all the energy evaporated from my body. "I think she's wasting her time. And," he leaned forward. "She's not honest with you or anybody else."

What?

My heart hammered against my ribs.

"What do you mean?" Aai asked, glancing between me and him.

"Now that we're talking, I don't see any harm in mentioning that," he waved his hand between us. "She doesn't care about this marriage."

Baba's eyes snapped to me. I kept my head low, eyes on my lap. My fingers shook. A chill ran through my spine.

"In fact," he nodded at Nishant. "I think something's going on between these two. The way she was dancing with him. The way she looks at him. No wonder she doesn't want to move closer to me. He's keeping her here."

The nerves on this boy are frightening. If the ground could tear and swallow me whole, Ankit would probably grip me and pull me up to humiliate me even more.

He met my father's eyes with confidence, "Come on, Sudhir Kaka. You of all people should notice all these things."

Oh my god.

He went too far insulting my father in front of everyone.

"Hey man, chill," Vihaan said. "This isn't the place to talk these things."

Ankit ignored him. He went ahead, saying, "I'm sorry to have done this here, but I waited enough for her to show some sort of commitment to me. She hasn't so far. And no matter how much I try, she doesn't want to be with me."

He looked me in the eyes. "You think I didn't notice?"

The world shrank upon me. I recoiled within myself, scared to even meet anyone's eyes, especially Nishant's. He was being dragged into the whole mess even when he had nothing to do with it. I risked stealing a glance at him. He was throwing a dagger stare at Ankit. His eyes softened when he saw me.

"That's enough for today," Vihaan stepped up again to defend me.

"Stay out of this," Ankit snapped. "None of your business."

"She's my sister," Vihaan countered. "So *it is* my business. It's all of our business. So you know what? You should leave."

"Who the hell are you to tell me to leave?"

"Stop it!" I screamed. Tears streamed down my face. "Ankit, please stop! Why are you doing this? You can't talk to my family like this. And for the last time, I don't want your help with the shop. I can handle it myself. And yes," I took a shaky breath. "It's true. I don't want to marry you. Not now, not ever!"

Ankit flinched at my words. His eyes darkened. A flicker of hurt flashed in his eyes, quickly replaced by cold anger.

Gathering all the strength I was left with, I pointed at the path ahead, "Please, just go!"

I didn't wait for him to leave as I stormed out of the party, heading straight home. My cheeks stung with a cold breeze. I shivered at the thought of answering my parent's questions.

I wasn't being truthful to myself and to my parents.

No. That's not how it was supposed to go. He ruined everything. That too on an evening I was most looking forward to. And oh god. Nishant. What must he think of me? How I'll ever face him again.

Reaching my apartment, I fumbled with the keys as I unlocked the door and stumbled inside. The safety of my home did little to soothe the storm raging within me.

Sinking onto the bed, I pulled the covers over my head, shutting out the world. My tears had dried, leaving a hollowness in my chest.

A soft knock at the door startled me. I turned around to see Avni and Rutu peeking through the door. "Can we come in?" Avni asked.

I only hummed in response.

Rutu sat beside me, soothingly running her fingers through my hair. "Are you okay?" she whispered.

I burst into tears all over again. All the hurt, anger, and humiliation came pouring out. I confessed everything – about Ankit, about fear of disappointing my parents.

Avni and Rutu listened patiently, exchanging sympathetic glances.

"It's all my fault," I finally choked out. "I ruined everything. How will I ever face Baba and Aai? And Nishant... what must he think of me?"

Avni pulled me into a warm hug. "Hey," she murmured. "It's not your fault. Ankit was out of line, and you had every right to stand up for yourself and your dreams."

"And don't worry. Nobody is mad at you," Rutu firmly added.

"And about Nishant," Avni pulled back, wiping my tears. "I assure you he's not gonna judge you."

"How do you know for sure?" I asked.

"I just know," she simply replied. I rested my head on her shoulder and she held me, stroking my arm to make me feel at ease.

The weight of the situation hadn't vanished entirely, but their presence made it a little easier. There would be consequences, difficult conversations, and maybe even heartbreak. But I'm ready to face it.

SEVENTEEN

I jerked awake, gasping for air. The hammering in my head intensified, making me dizzy, forcing me to lean my head on the window frame. I reached for a bottle of water on my nightstand and gulped long sips. It took me a while to adjust my vision to the darkness. Sunrise was still a couple of hours away.

Pulling my blanket to my chest, I felt as empty as the lane outside. Events of last night lined up to torture me. I closed my eyes and tried to focus on my breathing to calm my heartbeat.

Ankit's words kept flashing in my mind. Baba's distressed face. Aai's confused look. A whole new wave of humiliation surged through me. How could I have messed up everything so badly? I wish I had signed the contract for the new shop and paid the deposit. I wished I had told my parents about Ankit. I wished and wished, wondering if I could turn the time back to handle this differently. Keeping things unsaid only made it worse.

Unable to find peace, I threw my blanket aside and went into the living room lit by a small ceiling lamp.

To my surprise, Baba was seated on the couch, reading. He sensed my arrival and closed the book. "Couldn't sleep?" he asked, patting the space beside him. I settled onto the couch, resting my head on his shoulder.

"No," I mumbled. "You?"

He placed the book aside and removed his glasses. "No."

I am a horrible daughter. My parents shouldn't be losing sleep over the mess I created. They should enjoy their retirement without worrying about anything. And yet, I caused so much discomfort in their lives.

"Baba?"

"Hm?"

"Are you mad at me?"

He sighed, resting his cheek on my head. "Honestly? A little." His disappointment stung deep within my heart.

Hearing our murmur, Aai came outside, yawning and rubbing her eyes.

"I'm sorry," I said to both. "I have no excuse."

Baba shifted in his seat to face me. The knot in my stomach tightened. I braced myself, ready to hear whatever he had to say. I owed it to my parents.

"You're hiding important things from us. You don't want to marry Ankit? And we got to know about it from him. What happened to our open communication, Nupur? What did we do to lose our daughter's trust?"

My heart squeezed and eyes watered.

"Sudhir!" Aai said in a soft tone. "She's tired."

"No, Mahima," he said firmly. "She must answer my question."

My heart began to race. Baba was hurt. I couldn't look into his eyes.

"You were this tall," he raised his hand to the height of a tea table. "When you started talking to us. You'd tell us every minor detail of your life. And we understand that kids start living their own lives when they grow up, but still, you never hide things from us. Do you think we're getting old and can't help you anymore?"

That broke my heart. Tears traced a path down my cheeks. "No Baba. That's not what I think at all. I just didn't want you to..."

"Worry?"

I nodded.

"Worrying about our child is the only thing we parents want, Nupur. No matter how much you grow up. If you try to distance yourself from us, thinking we're old and you'd rather not bother us, you're stealing the only purpose of our lives."

I covered my face with my palms and closed my eyes. I never thought about it from their perspective. Ever since Baba retired, our roles somehow reversed in my mind. Now I take care of them the way they did for me while growing up. They're my responsibility and not the other way around.

Watching your parents grow old is never easy.

Aai's gentle tone broke the silence. "Why didn't you tell us, Nupur?"

"I was going to. I kept putting it off." I tucked my legs beneath me and leaned against the couch. "I thought it'd ruin our relationship with his family. Baba and Vikram Kaka are best friends. I didn't want to be the reason to break what they had cherished for years. But Ankit..."

I stole a glance at Baba, he was intensely listening to me. "What did he do?" he asked, frowning.

Dropping my gaze to my interlinked fingers, I decided to tell them the whole truth. How he broke all ties with me when he went to London and returned a changed man, how he talks down on me, and his lifestyle doesn't align with mine anymore.

"And I'm not sure yet, but you should also know that there's a girl named Priya. Maybe his girlfriend, I don't know. But.." I told them what I saw and how he reacted when I confronted him. The weight on my chest eased as I spilled everything I had bottled up for days.

"That's not good," Baba mumbled, rubbing his hand on his neck.

"I'm sorry," I said again. "I should've told you earlier."

Aai joined us on the couch. She held my hand in hers and softly smiled. "You can tell us anything, Nupur. Even if it's difficult."

I hugged her. "I will."

Slightly calmer than before, we talked about how to break the news to Ankit's parents. I hated the thought of making Nina Kaki cry. It'll break her heart. If there was a way to delicately handle it, it was long closed. Ankit probably went home last night and fed them a different narrative difficult for us to break. But, we had to be honest with them.

As the golden glow of sunrise trickled into the house, Aai went into the kitchen to make some tea. I drew the curtains and opened the balcony door to welcome the sunshine into our house.

"Nupur," Baba called from the couch. I tied the curtains and returned to him.

"Yes, Baba?"

Hesitantly, he asked, "Is it true what Ankit said? About Nishant?"

My heart lurched, but I didn't want to lie again. "I don't know, Baba. Maybe?"

He nodded. "Ok. We're here, your Aai and I. Whenever you want to talk about it." Being a tough policeman, my father may look strict from the outside. But his heart? Soft as his favorite red velvet cake. Softer still when it comes to his daughter.

"Thank you, Baba," I replied, relieved.

A beat of comfortable silence passed between us before he added, "We're sorry too, you know. We were so caught up in our little world, assuming you were happy. We should've asked your opinion."

"It's not your fault, Baba," I assured him. "Ankit...well, he changed. I always thought he loved me but maybe he never did. Whatever we had when we were teenagers was probably just a phase for him." My heart broke for my teenage self.

"I understand. Don't worry I'll talk to Vikram."

"Initially I thought he changed because he went away. Lived a different life. And I'm not against change, as long as it's good change. And isn't it in our hands how we choose to be as people for ourselves and others?"

Baba nodded. "Absolutely. And if he doesn't respect others, I'd rather lose my friendship with Vikram than be a reason behind my daughter's sadness."

"Thank you, Baba," I hugged him tighter, wiping my eyes to the sleeve of his shirt.

Aai brought the tray of tea into the living room. Sharing a cup of ginger tea together was comforting and refreshing.

"I'll go meet Vikram," Baba declared after finishing his tea. "No point delaying the conversation."

I panicked. "Baba. You can't go on your own. Should I come too?"

He shook his head. "No. It should just be me and him. Don't worry."

I looked at Aai for help. She only blinked.

When Baba went to his room to get ready, Aai collected all the empty tea cups in a tray. "Go take a shower, Nupur. I'll make some breakfast."

"Aai. Do you think it's a good idea? Baba going there alone?"

"They're best friends, Nupur. Don't worry. Let them figure it out first then we can join in later."

I decided to believe her and prayed that Baba wouldn't end up losing his best friend in the process.

"Okay," I mumbled, heading back to my room to take a long shower. Standing underneath a hot stream of water felt soothing to my skin. I let it wash away all the tiredness, insecurities, and uncertainties.

Tears rolled down my cheeks, blending into the water. I allowed myself to fall apart one last time. *I have a lot to figure out later.*

EIGHTEEN

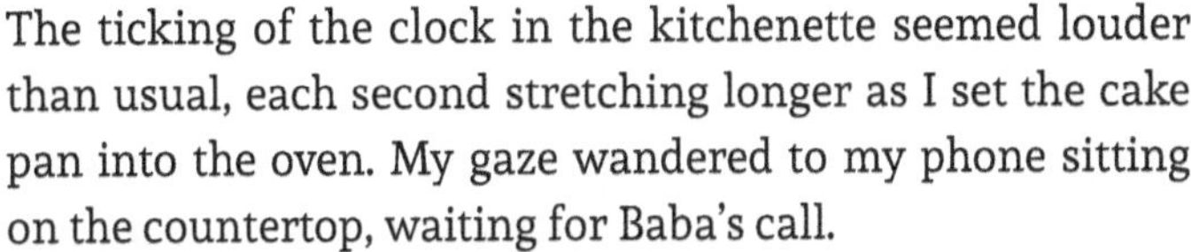

The ticking of the clock in the kitchenette seemed louder than usual, each second stretching longer as I set the cake pan into the oven. My gaze wandered to my phone sitting on the countertop, waiting for Baba's call.

He left to meet Vikram Kaka about two hours ago and I haven't been calm ever since. My mind played all kinds of scenarios, making my stomach churn with unease. I've been trying to distract myself with work, my last day of baking in a shop that had become a second home. I wanted to enjoy my last baking experience in this kitchenette. How could I when everything's falling apart?

Saying goodbye to this shop and returning the keys to Dixit Ajoba won't be easy. Soon I'll have to pack and move. For that, I must resume searching for a new shop.

Thoughts spiraled around me, suffocating me. I sank onto the chair. For the first time, baking failed to soothe me. I closed my eyes, desperately trying to sort out the clutter in my mind.

The bell over the door jingled, shattering the silence, and jolting me to stand up.

"Baba?" I called, sprinting out of the kitchenette. No. It was Rutu and Avni.

The girls paused in their tracks, exchanging a confused look.

"What's going on?" Rutu asked, her eyebrows furrowed.

"Nothing," I responded with a shaky breath.

"Come, let's sit outside for a while," she suggested.

I aimlessly followed the girls out and settled on the pavement steps outside the shop. That's when I noticed a thermos and paper cups in Avni's hands. She smiled and passed the cups to us, pouring refreshing lemongrass tea. The first sip had me lean into the warmth. The presence of my best friends eased me. "Thanks, Avni."

"Anytime," she replied.

Rutu set her empty cup aside and turned to face me, "Why didn't you tell us about Ankit, Nupur?" Her voice gentle and eyes soft. "No wonder you never wanted us to meet him."

"I don't know," I confessed. "I was scared, I guess. I loved him once. Wanted to marry him. And now when our parents are making it happen, I don't want to marry him anymore. He changed a lot and that's not the kind of person I want to marry. I just..." I trailed off.

"He's a disaster," Avni shook her head. "We're glad you and him are over."

"We were over the day he left for London. I just didn't see it until later." My heart ached recalling memories of those days. I never told anyone how heartbroken I was. Not even to my best friends. I wasn't ready to accept how much it affected me. How naive I was to think he'd miss me, remember me, tell his friends about a girl he couldn't wait to return to. Instead, he flicked a switch and forgot I even existed.

"His loss," Rutu declared. "Now chin up," she lifted my chin with her fingers. "Forget about him. Let's find you a new shop."

"Yes," I sighed, passing my phone to Rutu and Avni. "I found a few more shops about 5 km from here. Take a look. My only concern is the rent and size."

Girls scrolled through my list, browsing the pictures. "All the shops look good," Avni offered. "The third one is the closest."

"I'm planning to go see them all tomorrow itself. I'll take Baba with me."

"That sounds good. Let us know if you want us along," Rutu said with a smile.

"Thanks a ton, both of you." I'd be lost without these two girls.

"Don't thank us," Rutu held my gaze sharply and scolded me. "Just don't forget you don't have to hide things from us, especially if someone's bothering you."

"Promise," I smiled, grateful to have these two in my life.

Girls stayed with me for a while, distracting me by showing some of our pictures from the party. Even though the party sucked after Ankit arrived, I refused to let that bother me. Not anymore. It was a great party. We had so much fun. The pictures were good. We shortlisted a few, edited them, and posted them on Instagram while we shared a piece of blueberry cake.

"Did you see Mrs. Rane's dance?" Rutu giggled. "She was having fun, after all the drama she created."

I laughed. "Yes. I think she just wanted attention."

"I'm just glad the party was a success," Avni said. "A much-needed break for all of us..." she sighed, then added, "You know what? We should do something fun. Just the three of us."

"We should plan a movie night again," Rutu suggested, scooping another bite of cake.

"Yeah," Avni perked up, licking her spoon. "But not at my place. Last time when we all watched *Princess Diaries* with Nidhi, Tanvi Vahini was mad at me. I forgot to help Nidhi finish her homework and she was late for school the next day," she giggled.

"She was mad at us too," I laughed.

"We can go to the theatre for a change. We'll go to the mall. Watch a movie. Shop and eat until our tummies burst," Avni said, tossing her hair back.

"God. That sounds tempting," I replied. "We haven't had a day off like that in ages. Once I move into a new shop, we'll plan something"

"Done!" she beamed.

Giving me a bear hug, the girls went back to their shops. By that time, the cake was done. I kept it on the cooling rack and prepared a fresh batch of buttercream. I still had no idea where I'd move the cabinets, the display case, and my ovens until I find a new shop. Can't take them home. Where do I even begin to sort this mess?

No. I don't want to think about it today.

I promised myself a beautiful day in the shop and that's what I did. I spent the rest of the morning cleaning the display case, rearranging the cakes, snapping pictures, and greeting customers.

Then I closed orders on my website and food delivery apps, and posted an update on my Instagram that Baking Magic will be relocated soon and will only accept small orders until further updates.

As lunchtime approached, I checked my phone for any message from Baba. Knowing how anxious I must have been, he had sent a short message.

Baba: I'll be home in a few hours. Having lunch with Vikram. Nothing to worry about :)

I sighed and was about to set my phone aside when Nishant's new message blinked at me.

Nishant: Hey. Can we meet?

My heart skipped a beat. I wanted to see him. Needed to talk to him, to apologize on Ankit's behalf.

Hesitantly, I typed a reply and sent- *Hey. Sure, let me know when.*

A whole new train of thought began marching in my head. I hated feeling so out of control. Until a month ago, my life was set in an everyday loop. I'd wake up, open the shop, bake and sell cakes, and close the shop with satisfaction. A routine I never got tired of. That's what I always wanted. A sudden glitch in my routine was expanding day by day. I needed to stop it.

I pulled the cake stand in front of me and propped the freshly baked cake on it. Mixing the buttercream one more time, I began icing the cake, separating myself from the world outside that door. I know I can't tiptoe around everything. I'll have to carefully navigate through all the chaos without bruising my heart again.

With a last swirl of the piping bag across the edge of the cake, I kept it in the display case and checked the time. It was almost 2 o'clock. Aai must be waiting for me. Flipping the door sign to *Closed*, I locked the shop and went upstairs.

The scent of simmering tomato soup and steaming vegetable pulav drifted towards me.

"Is that basil I smell in the soup?" I asked.

"It is," she warmly smiled, garnishing the soup with fresh cream.

"Looks delicious."

The two of us sat on the couch, sharing a meal in front of the TV. Aai must be worried too, waiting for Baba's call since the morning. For my sake, she avoided all stressful topics. Instead, she distracted me with a piece of gossip about my aunt that had us both chuckling. I was grateful for the distraction. I wondered if she was sad. She was so excited to plan my wedding. She and Ankit's mother were constantly sharing ideas. I wanted to know what she was thinking now that the wedding was off.

"Aai?"

"Hm?"

"Are you upset with me?"

She gently placed her hand on mine and said, "No, Nupur. I'm not."

"Still, I'm sorry. I know how excited you were to plan my wedding."

She gave me a sad smile. "Not at the cost of your happiness, Nupur."

I pressed my lips together, "Will Nina Kaki be mad at me? She'll never talk to me again."

"No no," she said, shaking her head. "Nina adores you. She's not going to be mad at you. Nobody is."

"This is all so...difficult."

"Relationships are never easy, Nupur," Aai delicately said. "We just try our best to hold on to people. Don't worry, it'll all be fine."

I believed her.

"Anyway," she smiled, patting my cheek. "I'd rather celebrate your success. Wedding will happen whenever you're ready."

I leaned my cheek into her palm. "Thank you, Aai."

As we finished our lunch and washed the dishes, the doorbell rang.

"Must be Baba," Aai said.

"I'll check." I swung open the door and stopped short.

Girija Kaki stood in front of me with a nervous smile on her face.

NINETEEN

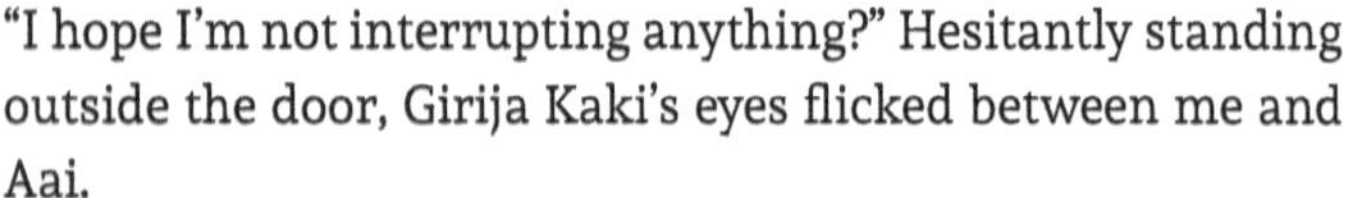

"I hope I'm not interrupting anything?" Hesitantly standing outside the door, Girija Kaki's eyes flicked between me and Aai.

"No, of course not, Kaki. Come on in," I stepped aside, ushering her in. She settled on the armchair in the living room. My mother and I were both surprised and delighted to see her. I couldn't even recall the last time she had visited our house. Feels like a lifetime ago.

"Would you like some soup, Girija? Have you had lunch?" Aai asked.

"Yes, I just ate. Thanks, Mahima," she replied softly.

"Some chai then?" Aai asked.

"Maybe later." Her gaze curiously swept across the living room. "Everything is so different now. You used to have cane furniture before this."

Aai's smile turned nostalgic. "You remember that?"

"We picked it together," Girija Kaki recalled. "Remember that exhibition you, me, and Amrita went to?"

My mother enthusiastically bobbed her head, "I do. They still host that exhibition every summer. We should go this year."

"Certainly." She shifted in the chair. Her eyes drifted towards me. She softly smiled and asked, "How are you, Nupur?"

"If you mean about last night, I'm better now. Sorry, you had to see that."

She waved off my embarrassment. "I'm glad it happened in front of us. That boy doesn't deserve you."

"That's true," Aai agreed. "We're still sort of processing the whole thing."

"I understand," Girija Kaki nodded, thoughtfully. "Is this a good time then? Or should I come back later?"

"No no, Girija. Please tell us how we can help you?"

Girija Kaki interlocked her fingers and rested her hands on her lap. "The reason I came here is..." she paused and met my gaze. "I'm sorry I wasn't very kind to you when you first came to my house asking for my shop."

My mother's brows furrowed in surprise. "When did this happen, Nupur? You never mentioned this."

"Sorry, Aai. It was the day after the dinner at PunePalette. Dixit Ajoba suggested...but," I trailed off.

Girija Kaki's shoulders slumped slightly. She finished my sentence for me. "But I refused her request. In fact," she continued, her lips pressed into a thin line, "I wasn't polite. I'm sorry I haven't been myself lately."

"It's okay, Girija Kaki. You don't have to apologize," I offered with a comforting smile.

Girija Kaki looked quite composed now. Her nervousness was all gone. Her voice was much warmer and comfortable.

"Anyway," she said. "You can rent out my shop anytime you want."

It took me a moment to register her words. She was offering me her shop. A perfect location for Baking Magic. A shop on Rhythm Lane. The shop she said she didn't want to rent out.

"Kaki, you don't have to do anything you're not comfortable with. I know you had your reasons to refuse my request earlier," I said, remembering how uncomfortable she was when I went to inquire about her shop.

"Yes," she admitted, her tone tinged with sadness. "I had my reasons. But none of that matters now. The shop is going to be empty, and you need it. I'd be a terrible neighbor if I don't let you use my shop after everything you people did for me."

Her voice cracked a little. She blinked several times, trying to push back tears pooling across the rim of her eyes. Aai and I both noticed it at the same time.

Aai couldn't hold back her concern after seeing the pain in her best friend's eyes. "Girija, what's going on? As your old friend, I want to know if you're okay."

Girija Kaki leaned back, taking a moment to reply. "I'm okay, Mahima. A lot happened over the years. I'm still getting used to certain things."

"Understandable," Aai said. "How's everyone? And Sanika?" She asked delicately.

"She's fine," Girija Kaki murmured. Her face remained stoic. "Working in Bangalore." Her reluctance to talk about her daughter was still visible in her eyes.

"Why don't you ask her to take a week off and spend it here with you?" Aai suggested.

She sighed. She looked like she wanted to say a lot but couldn't form words. She needed a safe space to open up and I wanted her to feel comfortable with us. "Girija Kaki, you don't have to tell us anything. But please know that, if you want to, we're here to listen and help."

She nodded silently. She gazed out through the balcony for a moment, lost in thought, her fingers nervously tracing patterns on her lap. The silence stretched, so many unspoken emotions, until finally, Girija Kaki spoke, her voice cracking ever so slightly.

"Years ago," she began. "When Sanika was just a teenager, we used to make ceramic plates and pots together. We'd paint them, hang them on the walls, create all sorts of crafts," she looked at me. "You remember that, don't you Nupur? You kids used to join us."

"I do, Kaki," I smiled warmly at the memory. Girija Kaki would patiently explain how to knead the clay, how to center the clay when the wheel begins to spin, and how to shape it into a pot. Our tiny muddy hands would try to keep up with her instructions. She'd hold a wet sponge to smoothen the edges and run a thread between the wheel and the clay to separate the pot. We would impatiently wait for it to dry so we could paint it with her.

"Sanika loved it as much as I did," she confessed. "She'd say- 'Aai, we'll make lots of ceramic pots in our studio and sell it in our own shop. And we'll also teach people who are interested in learning. Wouldn't it be fun?' and I hung on to that dream for a long time." She dabbed her tears with her handkerchief.

Aai and I remained silent, letting her share the thoughts she'd been bottling up for a long time.

She continued, "We'd talk about it all the time. Back then, the shop was always rented out, but our plan was to start something of our own."

"Then what happened?" I couldn't stop myself from asking.

"Then life happened," a sad chuckle escaped her lips. "Well, you all know about my husband. That was the biggest blow to overcome. Both financially and emotionally. Though he was proven not guilty, the whole experience changed Avdhut. He is a different person now, almost a stranger."

My heart ached as I listened. What must they have gone through during those tough times? I could only imagine.

"How is he?" Aai asked.

"He's okay," Girija Kaki replied. "He lives on his parent's farm in Ratnagiri. I think Avdhut couldn't get out of that fear. He never spoke about it. And we sort of drifted apart without realizing it." She continued, "I needed the support of my family, and Sanika needed a stable environment, so I thought it'd be better to move closer to my family in Satara. But looking back, maybe I made a mistake prioritizing my needs over hers."

"What do you mean?" Aai frowned.

Girija Kaki's eyes darkened as she recalled, "Sanika begged me and Avdhut to stay on Rhythm Lane. She loved it here. This was her home, she said. But I was clouded by my own insecurities and Avdhut was, well....he was scared. So I just ignored Sanika's needs and insisted we move closer to my family. Avdhut and I made that decision together and Sanika wasn't happy about it. She'd spend her summer holidays with Avdhut, but...it was never the same."

The weight of Girija Kaki's words hung heavy in the air. The silence in the room extended for a long moment.

"She felt trapped," Girija Kaki murmured. "So, she left as far away as she could. Got a job in Bangalore. A stable life. She sends me money every month, takes care of me from afar, but..." Tears escaped her eyes. Aai immediately reached out and squeezed her hand to comfort her.

Girija Kaki drew a deep breath and wiped her eyes. "This whole situation changed her a lot too. She grew up way before her age. Before coming to stay here again, I asked her if she'd consider coming back home and starting our long-due business?" Another stream of tears cascaded down her cheeks. "But she thinks it's silly. She said we need financial security and she's right. But I wasn't over our dream. It was the only thing that kept me going after everything that happened. Now seemed like a correct time but..." Girija Kaki paused. She looked at my mother and said. "She has a boyfriend now. She wants to get married and settle down. I haven't even met him yet."

"But you'll meet him, right?" Aai asked.

"I suppose," she said. "But instead of showing my support, I argued and said things I can never take back. In the heat of our argument, I told her to not come back, that she can get married on her own and settle wherever she wants," a sob shook her shoulders. I shifted closer to her and pulled her into a hug.

"It's okay, Girija Kaki," I held her close. "We're here for you now. And Sanika... she won't be mad at you."

She sniffled, clinging to me. Aai gently rubbed her back. "Don't worry, Girija. Everything will be okay."

Girija Kaki allowed herself to fall apart. Aai and I never left her side as she slowly recovered. "I didn't come here to cry," she said after a while, wiping her tears. "I don't think I need that shop. But if you can use it, I'd be happy. At least your dreams can continue if not ours."

I looked at Aai. Her eyes watered for her friend.

Girija Kaki held my hands in hers. "Please, Nupur. I know I was rude to you but I truly mean it. I want you to have that shop."

"Kaki, it'd be a great help for me."

"Then take it," she said again, more firmly this time. "Otherwise it'll be of no use to anyone. In fact, Mr. Dixit left a glorious recommendation for you. You're the best tenant one could have, his words."

I chuckled, "He's sweet."

"You sure, Girija?" Aai asked. "Do you want to ask Sanika first?"

"Sanika won't mind, I assure you," she replied, firmly.

Tears welled up in my own eyes. I blinked them away and smiled, "Girija Kaki, you have no idea how big of a help that would be. I can't thank you enough."

"I'm glad I could be of any use to anyone. I've proven myself to be useless to my daughter."

"Don't say that, Girija," Aai gently said. "Sanika won't be mad at you for long. She'll come back."

"I doubt it. I was very firm when I told her never to return."

"It's just a fight, Girija Kaki. Aai and I fight all the time. I'm sure Sanika won't be mad at you for long. I think you should call her. Tell her to come back."

She pulled back, a flicker of doubt clouding her teary eyes. "What if she doesn't?"

"She will," I said. "You have to try. Maybe she misses you just as much."

"Nupur is right, Girija. Give her a call," Aai added. "I'm sure she'll want to see you."

Girija Kaki seemed to consider our suggestion. With a glimmer of hope in her eyes, she finally spoke, "You're right. I should call my daughter."

A small smile returned to her lips after a long silence. "Thank you for listening to me." She brushed her fingers over my cheeks. "And thanks for looking after me. You welcomed me back into the neighborhood, I'm grateful for that."

"You're family, Girija Kaki".

She smiled. "So? You'll take the shop?"

I hugged her. "Thank you, Kaki. Yes, I'm more than happy to. You're saving me a lot of trouble."

She patted my back. "It's settled then."

"Let me bring some sweets," Aai said, disappearing into the kitchen. "Would you like to spend some more time here, Girija?" she suggested. "I'll call Amrita. We can catch up some more."

"I'd like that," she replied with a smile so warm, I knew she was finally back.

TWENTY

Rhythm Lane has always held me close in a warm embrace. I've been surrounded by loving people ever since I came here. My friends, neighbors, they're my family. How could I forget even for a second that I'm never alone? I'm grateful for having so many people by my side.

Not a single person who witnessed Ankit's outburst at the party reminded me of it. Everyone's determined to make me forget it. Especially Baba, who kept telling me I had nothing to worry about. He and Vikram Kaka talked it through and decided to stay friends. I don't fully believe him, but I didn't have time to think about it at all.

I received so many helping hands as I closed my shop and shifted most of my equipment in my room. Thanks to Avni, my display case and shelves found a place to stay for a few days in her book cafe. I would have preferred not to close my shop even for a week. But the timeline couldn't match no matter how hard I tried.

Handing over the keys to Dixit Ajoba brought tears to my eyes and his too. He was leaving Pune for good, and he wanted to meet everyone before he left. I packed lots of cookies and brownies for him and a dozen cupcakes for his grandkids. His whole face lit up when I told him that Girija Kaki agreed and thanked him for putting in a good word for me. "I'm glad I could help!"

"Thank you so much, Ajoba."

"Stay in touch, beti. And my best wishes are always with you," he kept his palm on my head as a blessing. As always, I accompanied him until he was settled in a Rikshaw and waved goodbye.

After having dinner with my parents, I buckled a bunch of cleaning equipment and a portable lamp to my Scooty and drove to the empty shop with streetlights filtering through the window. Piling up my hair in a messy bun, I looked around, picturing my Pinterest board come to life.

The shop is bigger than my previous one, with room for cozy seating to enjoy a cup of coffee and desserts. A charming patio can be converted into outdoor seating. A matching canopy will go above the glass door and the large window frame, decorated with fairy lights and flowers. It'll be gorgeous.

Balancing on the ladder, I began dusting the walls and the ceiling. My parents and even Girija Kaki insisted on helping, but I sent them away. Everyone's helped me enough. I needed to do this on my own.

Carefully, I climbed the ladder, balancing myself. My legs trembled a little as I tiptoed to reach the corners of the ceiling. Gripping the frame of the ladder in one hand and the broom in the other, I got rid of the spider webs and dust.

"Need a hand?" A soft voice floated through the doorway, making my head turn and my heart jump. Nishant leaned against the doorframe with his arms folded over his chest. A glint in his beautiful eyes was shiny enough to make the whole room glow.

Though we exchanged a few messages over the past couple of days, we haven't had a chance to meet, and I won't lie, I was nervous to face him.

"Hey," I managed a steady tone. "Come on in."

I climbed off the ladder and rested the broom by the wall.

He stepped inside with his hands in his pockets and scanned the shop. "This is nice," he smiled.

"Thanks." I wiped my hands on my pants and pulled off my dust mask. "You're leaving late?"

He shrugged, "Had tons of work. Ended up grabbing dinner with Vihaan and Avni."

"How's it going? Your work?" He knew I was avoiding discussing the party incident. I could feel it in his body language. I couldn't meet his gaze without remembering his expression when Ankit insulted everyone, including him.

Sensing my anxiety, he stepped closer, his voice gentle. "Nupur, I know it's bothering you. But I need you to know that it's not your fault."

"It *is* my fault," I mumbled, looking away. "I should've been more honest with...well, myself. I'm sorry he dragged you into the mess. You didn't deserve to be humiliated like that."

He sighed and ran his fingers through his hair. "I'm not humiliated, Nupur. You shouldn't feel that way either."

I sat on the flat step of the ladder and perched my hands on my knees. "But I do. It shouldn't have happened like that. And I'm truly sorry."

"You don't have to apologize to anyone," he said, holding my gaze.

"So, you're not upset with me?" I asked.

"I never was, Nupur," his voice softened.

Relief washed over my earlier distress. "Thank you," I murmured.

"Don't worry about anything," he said, shuffling a little closer.

I nodded. He looked at me with so much concern, his eyes talked more than his words could. He waited for my response.

"Yes. I'm okay now," I replied, genuinely.

A soft smile tugged at his lips. He rolled his sleeves over his bicep and rubbed his palms together. "Alright. How can I help?"

I tapped my finger on my chin, examining the shop. It looked much cleaner, though I'll do another round of cleaning tomorrow before I start painting it.

My eyes landed on an old heavy metal table standing awkwardly next to the window. I couldn't move it an inch when I tried.

"I do need help moving that monstrosity," I nodded at the table. "I tried pushing it to the corner but it wouldn't budge."

Nishant leaned his head back and laughed. A sound so enchanting, I felt it buzzing through my veins. I watched him lift the table from one end and effortlessly drag it aside. His muscles flexed as he pushed it to the corner and dusted his hands.

"Anything else?"

There really wasn't anything for him to do. I had it under control. But I didn't want him to leave so soon.

"I only have to clean the loft real quick. If you don't mind waiting, we can leave together?"

"Sure. I'll wait." He looked at the loft, then at me. An eyebrow went up. "Umm, are you sure about that?" he chuckled.

"Yes, I have a ladder, don't worry," I rolled my eyes, grinning.

Dunking the mop in a bucket of water, I gripped the ladder and hoisted myself onto the first step. As I reached for the next step, the hem of my sweatpants tangled into the screw. My foot slipped, and I tripped over.

"Careful!" Nishant rushed to my side. A strong hand shot out, wrapping around my waist to pull me upright. My mop clattered to the floor and I found myself clinging to Nishant's shirt.

"Sorry," I mumbled.

His arm was still around my waist. A step closer and I'd be in his arms. His cologne was teasing me, urging me to bury my face under his jaw and let him hold me. I looked up to find his eyes on me. His gaze dropped to my lips just for a moment before he looked back at me. "You okay?"

"Yeah." It hurt to unclench his shirt and step away from him. I wish I could stay between his arms forever.

"Do you need water?" he asked, already fumbling in his backpack. "Here," he unscrewed his water bottle and handed it over.

"Thanks." I took a long sip and coughed.

He gently rubbed my back. "Maybe you should call it a day and start fresh tomorrow?"

"You're right."

We stumbled into each other's steps a couple of times before Nishant moved aside, freeing a path for me. He folded the ladder and slid it under the table while I cleaned the mop and left it resting by the wall.

Rolling down the metal door, I locked the shop and pocketed the keys. "Where's your bike?" I came to a halt, seeing him without his bike for the first time.

"In the garage," he replied, swinging his backpack over his shoulder. "Just regular servicing."

"Then how did you come here today?"

"Took the bus," he shrugged.

"Oh. I'll drop you at the bus stop then. My Scooty is parked aside, let me quickly get it."

Without waiting for his response, I brought my Scooty to the front of the shop. "Come on," I nodded towards the back seat.

He nervously glanced at me, debating his next move. "Do you mind if I drive?"

"Actually. I do."

He rubbed his neck, reluctant to consider my offer.

I laughed. "Relax, Nishant. You can trust me."

He dramatically joined his palms and looked up at the sky. "God, please save me today."

I swatted his shoulder. "Just hop on."

A chuckle left his lips as he settled on the backseat.

"Ready?"

"Do I have a choice?"

"Here we go," I started the engine and began riding towards the nearest bus stop, with Nishant clinging to his life in the backseat. I was giddy the whole five minutes of the ride.

"Thanks," Nishant hopped off as we reached. A small smile danced across his lips.

"Anytime," I parked my Scooty to the side of the bus stop.

"You don't have to wait," he said, checking the time on his phone. "I'll be fine."

"I want to," I smiled.

"You sure?"

"Positive."

So there we were, waiting for his bus. The sound of the buzzing city revolved around us. Nishant reached out and brushed the dust off a loose strand of my hair.

I looked down at my dirty clothes. "Gosh, I'm a mess."

"No, you're not." His voice was soft as a feather. A shiver trickled down my spine.

I didn't want the evening to end. Being near him was soothing, comforting. No judgments. No questions. Just us. He adjusted the straps of his backpack and glanced into the distance.

"There's my bus," he stepped forward as the bus halted near us. A bunch of people rushed to get inside. Nishant lingered behind. "Thanks for the ride, Nupur," he said, before getting in.

I nodded. "Anytime. Good night."

He found a seat by the window and looked outside, flashing a beautiful smile at me. I waved at him, watching the bus carry him away from me. The emptiness I felt after he left threw me off guard. I couldn't ignore my feelings for that man. Not anymore.

TWENTY-ONE

I floated through the first week of the new year with a roller paintbrush in my hand and paint stains on my pants. It was rewarding, exhausting, confusing, and everything in between. And honestly, I couldn't have asked for anything better to do. *Baking Magic* finally has a place to call home again and making it beautiful was my sole focus. My mind was buzzing with ideas and a thrill of anticipation.

It all began two days before New Year's Eve when Baba and I spent the whole day smoothening the walls with sandpaper. Baba made it look so easy that the cramps in my hand and shoulder were quite embarrassing.

"Come on, come on!" He'd tease, his voice booming through the shop. "No time for crying!"

Then we called an electrician to fix the wiring and got the lights working. No more portable lamps. The whole shop lit up with a flick of a button and I hadn't been this happy with electricity before. Later that afternoon, I applied the primer on the walls with the roller brush and ended up spraining my ankle in the process. No big deal.

On New Year's Eve, Aai, Baba, and I sat on the balcony, spreading out a rug and using my laptop to explore paint and decor combinations. Pastel pink and white was a clear winner. White floral decor, lacey white curtains, matching tables and chairs, and most importantly, a wall of memories where I'll showcase my favorite pictures with my friends, my family, and my happy customers. Everything was sketched from my dreamland.

We ordered Biryani and Mango Mastani shake topped with Mango ice cream for dessert and enjoyed our last dinner of the year on our balcony illuminated with fairy lights. After dinner, I iced the chocolate temptation cake and went to the garden of Avni's book café along with my parents. A bunch of us gathered to greet the new year together. We cut the cake as the fireworks danced across the sky at midnight.

The last month had been a roller coaster. A lot happened within a span of a few weeks that nearly crumbled up my hope. Now, my heart is filled with the promise of the new year with endless possibilities. I have so much to accomplish.

So, on the 1st of January, I dived into the shop makeover project. Girija Kaki, very kindly, gave me all the freedom to transform the shop the way I wanted. My excitement was through the roof as I dunked the roller brush in a tray of pastel pink paint and rolled it across the wall from the top edge to the bottom. With Sunidhi Chauhan's playlist in the background, I watched my shop take the color of my dreams. So satisfying.

The only other reason, besides saving money, for taking on the painting myself was the sheer pleasure of decorating it with my own hands. I've ordered some wall art stickers from Amazon that'll make these walls even prettier.

"Heya!" Rutu sang from the door, making her way into the shop with Avni by her side. Both wore ridiculous clothes to match my vibe with their hair piled up in a bun over their head.

"Wow. You've made so much progress," Avni said, taking a brush from the table and tossing one at Rutu. They were by my side, singing along.

"I'm taking this wall."

"I'll take this one."

The girls decided between themselves.

"What about your shops?" I asked, watching them happily dunk their roller brushes in the paint.

"No urgent orders," Rutu declared, loading her brush with paint. "Besides, your father volunteered to hold down the fort. He said he'd call if a customer stops by."

I chuckled. "Sounds like he misses managing the shop. What about you, Avni?"

"Aai is there. Tanvi Vahini offered to handle orders, so I kept everything ready in the kitchen. And," she giggled. "Nidhi is helping."

"Really?"

"Yup. She's started recommending books now. You should've seen her yesterday. She convinced a woman to buy a couple of children's books for her nephew."

"She's learning from the best," I grinned at her.

We hummed along to the songs as we painted the walls. Two hours felt like two minutes in a whirlwind of chatter, gossip, laughter, and singing with my best girls. The first coat of paint was done before I knew it.

"Thank you so much for helping," I pulled them into a hug, paint smudging across our clothes.

"It looks good," Rutu proudly smiled. "I can't wait to see how everything comes together. Though I'm gonna miss having you next door."

"Me too. But I'm glad I don't have to move away from this lane," I replied. It almost felt impossible a few weeks ago. Thanks to Girija Kaki, I'm only moving down the lane.

"That's true," she agreed. "But now I'm concerned about who's gonna be my new neighbor."

"Whoever it is, they should be more concerned," Avni laughed and bit her tongue as Rutu rolled her eyes.

"I'm sure you'll be fine," I said to Rutu, who shrugged.

"When's your wedding cake order due?" Avni asked, putting the brush down and wiping her hands and face with a paper towel.

"In two days."

All the fresh ingredients arrived this morning. Baking it at home will be tricky. The space isn't enough. But I'll manage.

"How exciting," Avni beamed. "All the best."

Leaning against the table, I untied my hair and ran my fingers through it to release some tension. "Thank you. I'm a little nervous, to be honest. Anything can go wrong with a four-layered wedding cake, especially assembling it without a crack."

I'd watched countless videos on cake assembly techniques, so hopefully, I was prepared.

"You'll do great," Rutu offered, confidently.

"Thank you so much."

"Call us if you need any help," Avni said. She and Rutu closed the lid of the paint containers while I cleared the table. I was tired and starving, and eager to bury myself in my blanket.

Avni threw her arm over my shoulder as we stepped out of the shop. "I'm so happy you got this shop, Nupur. Rutu and I would've missed you so much. We were really sad, you know?"

"I know. Even I was surprised when Girija Kaki offered. Then she told me why she refused to rent out her shop earlier and honestly, it's heartbreaking. But she's fine now and I hope she stays here with us."

"We didn't even know half the things that happened with them," Avni mumbled.

It pained me when we got to know the truth of Avdhut Kaka, who was wrongly accused and jailed. The shock of it all left him broken. He was innocent but the time he spent in jail and the humiliation ate up all of his existence. I couldn't even picture what it must have been like for him, his family, his daughter.

"We were too young to do anything then, but maybe we can do something now," I suggested.

"Like what?" Avni asked.

"Okay, so I tried to find Sanika through mutual friends as you suggested. And I may have found her on LinkedIn. I'm thinking of reaching out. What do you think?"

Rutu and Avni exchanged thoughtful glances. "There's no harm in texting her. She's our childhood friend after all," Avni said.

"Yes. I'll casually ping her tomorrow," I decided.

We lingered outside Rutu's shop, freeing my father from his duties. We sat on the steps and chatted away for a long time before going our separate ways. I was so exhausted, I walked like a zombie as I went upstairs, stuffed my tummy with a dal rice, and showered before embracing my comfortable bed.

It felt so nice to lie on my back. My body ached from all the extra physical work. I pulled my blanket over to my chest and let out a sigh of relief, feeling a deep sense of accomplishment. Closing my eyes, I drifted into a long dreamless sleep.

TWENTY-TWO

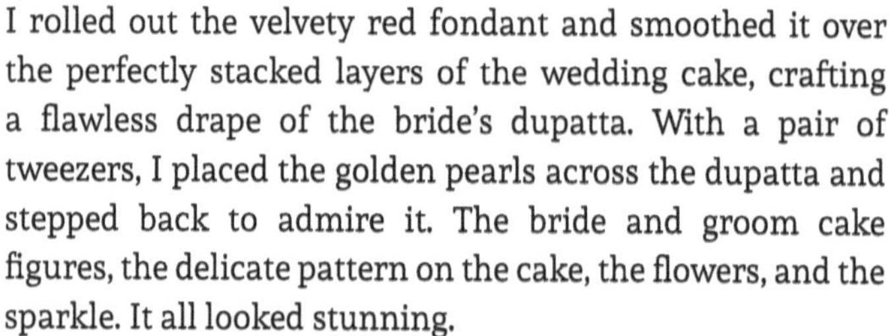

I rolled out the velvety red fondant and smoothed it over the perfectly stacked layers of the wedding cake, crafting a flawless drape of the bride's dupatta. With a pair of tweezers, I placed the golden pearls across the dupatta and stepped back to admire it. The bride and groom cake figures, the delicate pattern on the cake, the flowers, and the sparkle. It all looked stunning.

The massive, four-layered cake was finally ready, but delivering it would be an even bigger challenge, especially without Baba's presence. Ever since Baba left to meet Vikram Kaka again this afternoon, I haven't been at ease. I don't even know why Vikram Kaka called him again. When I asked, both Baba and Aai brushed my concern off. "Only to catch up, nothing to worry about," they both told me, avoiding eye contact. They were clearly lying, but I didn't push any further and decided to focus my entire attention on decorating the cake.

"Wow!" Aai exclaimed, gazing at the cake. "It looks amazing."

I smiled. "Thanks, Aai."

She patted my back and helped me pack the cake in a handmade insulated cardboard box lined with slip-free mats and ice packs. Carefully, with a silent prayer, I slid the cake into the case and secured it with tape.

"You're not gonna tell me, are you?" I asked, feeling restless. Baba never told me how his previous meeting with Vikram Kaka went. He never told me why he was called again. The fear of the unknown followed me like a shadow. "It'll be a lot easier for me to get on with the day if you just give me a hint."

Aai sighed. "Honestly, Nupur, I don't know the whole story. But trust me, there's nothing to worry about. Focus on the delivery. Baba will probably be back before you return."

"Okay." I gave up. The clock ticked away, reminding me of the deadline. I had to reach the venue on time.

The doorbell rang sharply at 5:30. "That must be Vihaan." When I asked Vihaan if he could drop me off at the venue in Ajoba's minivan, he didn't even hesitate before clearing his schedule. What did I do to deserve a brother like him?

I swung open the door, "I just need 2 minutes to change....oh!" and stopped with a jolt of surprise. Nishant, with his hair slicked back, stood on the doorstep with hands in his pocket.

"Hey. Vihaan has an urgent meeting. He asked me to drive you. Is that alright?"

"Yeah, sure." I paused. "But, do you have time? Otherwise, I can manage."

"I'm free. Don't worry about it."

Hearing his voice, my mother emerged into the living room. "Nishant beta, come on in," she said warmly. "Want some chai?"

"Umm..." he hesitated.

"I'm making chai for myself and Nupur anyway. Have some with us," my mother insisted, gesturing towards the couch. "Make yourself at home."

"Sure," he said. "Thanks Kaki."

I stepped aside to let him through. "I'll be back in two minutes." I hurried into my room, freeing my hair from a messy bun. Changing into a teal blue kurta paired with white jeans, I quickly ran a comb through my hair and applied light makeup. Gazing into the mirror one more time, I made my way back into the living room.

Nishant and my mother were engaged in a conversation over a cup of tea as I joined them, their laughter rising in the air. An unfamiliar warmth blossomed in my chest, a mixture of curiosity and something more I couldn't quite define. My mother wouldn't let him go before he ate at least one cookie with tea. Nishant's eyes found mine and he smiled.

"Ready to go?" he asked.

I glanced at the wall clock, "Yes, let's go."

He quickly arranged all our empty tea cups onto the tray.

"I'll do it, beta," my mother smiled at him.

"Thanks for the tea, Kaki. It was delicious."

Together, we carefully carried the cake box down through the elevator and loaded it into Chaturvedi Ajoba's minivan. I sat next to the box, clinging to it with my whole life.

"Nishant, drive very slowly," I requested, anxiously.

He offered a reassuring smile. "Don't worry." Buckling his seatbelt, he glanced back at me. "Relax."

I looked out the window, watching the buzz of the city pass by. As the familiar path unfolded ahead of us, I sent a quick text to Ananya to inform her I was on my way.

Nishant steadily navigated through the city. About twenty minutes later, he pulled the van to a halt just outside the venue's main gate, adorned with vibrant flower garlands, shimmering fairy lights, and a welcoming red carpet.

He unbuckled his seat belt and stepped out to open the door for me. The two of us carefully lifted the box and carried it inside.

Ananya, struggling to hold her saree pleats, hurried across the lawn to greet me. "Nupur, welcome! You're right on time." She turned to two of her volunteers hovering nearby. "Take this to the pantry, please." The two men took the box from us, kept it on a trolley, and rolled it to the pantry.

"Careful!" Ananya yelled behind them. Her gaze returned to me, filled with genuine appreciation. "Thanks so much for the timely delivery. Please, enjoy some snacks and refreshments. Do you have any final touches you need to make?"

"Just a quick check on the flower arrangement and the pearls," I replied.

"Alright." She pushed her glasses over the bridge of her nose and put a checkmark on her notepad next to the cake delivery. "I'll call you in a bit then." With that, she practically ran across the garden in her heels, busying herself in fixing the seating arrangement.

Turning back to Nishant. I let out a calming breath. "That went well," I declared, relaxing my tensed shoulders. "Let's grab something to eat, shall we?" I suggested, gesturing towards a nearby table.

"Sure," he readily agreed.

For the next half an hour, we enjoyed delicious food, lively music, and the vibrant chaos of the wedding guests.

As the clock neared 7 PM, Ananya reappeared, ushering me over to finalize the cake presentation. Nishant followed me, offering a helping hand to transfer the cake from the box to the glass table.

When the cake was finally revealed on stage, bathed in the sparkly glow of chandeliers, lanterns, and string lights, it looked even more dazzling than I had imagined. With a piping bag filled with frosting, I adjusted the edible flowers one last time. The drape of fondant shimmered like a bride's dupatta. I clicked a few pictures on my phone and stepped aside. Radhika, wearing a gorgeous red Lehenga Choli, walked to the stage with her hand looped into Abhay's. His off-white Sherwani with red embroidery complimented her Lehenga.

Fireworks erupted in the sky and cheers echoed as the bride and groom cut the cake together, sharing a first bite. I managed to capture this heartwarming moment on my phone, happy to be a part of such a special evening.

The pure joy in the bride and groom's eyes caught my attention. I tore my gaze from the phone screen to the happy couple on the stage. That's how it must look- *true love.*

"They look so beautiful together," I murmured, slipping my phone into my sling bag.

"True," Nishant whispered. "Look at their smiles."

So genuine and pure.

As the cake was taken away from the stage, guests began lining up to shower the newlyweds with blessings and gifts.

"Hey look," Nishant tapped my shoulder. "They're keeping the cake by the buffet. I wanna grab a bite."

Before I could respond, he made his way to the cake now being cut into bite-sized pieces. A queue formed in front of it. Nishant impatiently waited for his turn and managed to get a piece on a saucer along with two spoons.

"It's delicious. And soft," he declared, taking a bite. I allowed myself a tiny bite and was relieved as the sweetness of the soft spongy creation melted on my tongue.

Ananya, finally free from her hosting duties, approached me with a beaming smile. "Your cake is super hit, Nupur. I mean, look at the queue. Everyone's loving it, especially Radhika and Abhay."

My heart swelled with pride. "I'm so happy to hear that."

"I'd be honest," she said. "After my previous experiences with cake vendors, I was a bit nervous. But you delivered beyond expectations."

"I have to admit," I let out a nervous chuckle, "I was quite worried too."

She fist-bumped me. "We did good. If you're interested, I'd love for you to be my cake vendor for more events. What do you say? We make a great team."

A surge of excitement made my heart do a little cartwheel. "Really?"

"Of course," Ananya patted my shoulder. "I need someone like you on my team."

"I'd love to," I replied with equal enthusiasm.

She grinned at me. "Okay then, I'll be in touch."

"Anytime," I smiled back.

Shaking her hand, Nishant and I made our way to the parking. As we approached the van, Nishant gently patted my shoulder, "Wow. Kudos. That's a huge achievement."

"I know right?" Overwhelmed with joy, I flung my arms around him, consuming him in a tight hug. "I don't have words to tell you how happy I am. I always wanted this."

"You deserve it." His arms enveloped me. He swept me off the floor and spun me around. I giggled and held onto him a little longer when he set me back down. My face was still buried in the crook of his neck. A soft tickle of his warm breath on my neck pulled me back into reality.

I slowly drew back from him. My heart pounded in my chest.

"Um. Thanks," I mumbled, tucking the strand of my hair behind my ear. Gathering courage, I looked into his eyes. They lingered on my lips before flickering back to my eyes in a moment so raw, my heart skipped a beat.

I held his gaze despite the nervous wobble in my knees.

He ran a hand through his hair. "Let's get you home."

"Hm." I went around the van to the passenger seat. Nishant settled behind the wheel, peeking into the rearview mirror before bringing the van onto the road. We began driving home in silence. I tried to come up with something to say but couldn't think of anything. I fiddled with the radio in the van and synced it to the station that played 90's songs.

Navigating through the internal roads, we arrived on the highway. Streetlights outlined the path ahead. Vehicles moved at a steady pace. As we approached the exit by the hills, Nishant pulled the van aside and killed the engine. He stepped out and paced towards the front of the van. Confused, I followed him out.

It was cold out there. I rubbed my shoulders to stay warm as I stood next to him. "Why did you stop?"

He leaned against the van. One leg positioned in front of the other. Arms folded across his chest. "I can't do this anymore," he whispered into the cold evening air.

"What?"

He turned to face me. Waving his hand between us, he repeated, "I cannot do this anymore."

"Can't do what?"

"Pretend to be your friend," he replied, sounding overwhelmed.

I frowned, taken aback by his words. "What are you saying, Nishant?"

Hesitation flashed over his face. He drifted his eyes away from me, his voice low and intense. "I don't know how to say it."

"Did I do something?" I asked, getting anxious.

"No, of course not," he shook his head. "That's not it."

"Then what?"

Eyes still on the road ahead, he murmured. "I..."

"Just tell me, please."

His eyes landed on mine. He reached out to hold my hands and stepped a little closer. My heart began to race.

"I like you, Nupur," he said, holding my gaze. "Ever since I met you. When you brought cupcakes to Avni's cafe and smiled at me. I still remember that smile. My heart felt something that day. And initially, I thought I just liked you a normal amount. But no, I like you a whole lot more. I think I've fallen in love with you." A tiny smile appeared on his lips.

My heart was beating so loud, I thought I'd pass out. I wanted to say so many things, but words wouldn't form.

"I know you have a lot going on in your life, so I'm not expecting anything from you, Nupur. I just can't keep it in my heart anymore."

When I didn't utter a word, he continued, "I didn't know about Ankit. I thought you liked him but then the party incident happened and....look, I need you to know that I'm not just saying all these things. I mean it. You have no idea how scared I am right now."

My gaze dropped. "Me too."

"You're scared too?" he asked.

"A little bit."

"Why?"

"I don't know."

"It's okay," he said, brushing his thumb against my palm. So soft. So comforting. "I understand if you don't feel the same way."

"But I do," I blurted out.

His eyebrow went up. "You do?"

I nodded, stepping a little closer. A soft chuckle escaped his perfectly smiling lips. My cheeks warmed. Blush crept over me as I dared lacing my fingers with his. It felt so right. "It's a little complicated," I mumbled, looking at our intertwined hands. "I need some time to process everything."

"Take all the time you need," he said. "I'm not in a hurry."

A tiny tear managed to spill across my cheeks. He gently wiped it with his finger and opened his arms for me. Without a second thought, I allowed myself to melt into his arms. To forget the world exists outside the two of us. To inhale his scent and carry it with me. To let his heartbeats sync with mine.

He leaned against the van so I wouldn't have to raise my toes to hug him. My cheek brushed against his as I pulled back a little. His lips inches away from mine. Our eyes met. A silent confession passed between us before his lips gently touched mine. My eyelids fluttered close. My fingers went into his hair instinctively. He cupped my cheeks into his hands, softly kissing me and I kissed him back with all my heart.

As we pulled back, I rested my forehead on his, catching my breath.

"I don't want to go home yet," I confessed.

"Then we'll stay here for a while," he whispered, wrapping his arms around me.

My phone rang, crashing the beautiful moment. "Sorry, just a moment."

"No worries."

I fumbled to take my phone out of my purse. "Aai?"

"Um. Nupur, where are you?" she asked.

"On the way," I replied, glancing at Nishant who nodded, fishing keys out of his pockets.

Voices of Baba, Vikram Kaka, and Nina Kaki floated through the phone. My heart lurched to my throat. "Aai? What's going on?"

"Everything is okay," she assured me. "But you need to come home."

TWENTY-THREE

The elevator door slid open, revealing the quiet hallway of my apartment. The comfort of returning home to the familiar scent of coffee did nothing to ease the churning in my stomach. Clutching the strap of my sling bag, I made my way to the door already left open for me.

Four pairs of eyes turned in my direction. Concern creased around Nina Kaki's eyes and disappointment clouding Vikram Kaka's face intensified the knot in my stomach. I wasn't prepared to have this conversation.

I managed a thin smile despite my racing heart. My eyes flew to Aai, perched on the armchair next to Baba. She blinked and nodded at an empty chair set between her and Nina Kaki.

Dropping my sling bag to the floor, I hesitantly sat on the chair. "How are you, Kaki?"

Nina Kaki offered a strained smile, the kind that couldn't wipe off the sadness in her eyes. "I've been better," she replied.

I winced. The weight of her distress settled heavily on my shoulders. The entire room felt like it was collapsing upon me, suffocating me, smothering me. I concentrated on my breathing, waiting for someone to break the dreadful silence. Nervously glancing between Aai and Baba, I fiddled with the hem of my kurta.

A gentle touch on my hand startled me. Nina Kaki soothingly enveloped my hand in hers. "Calm down," she said, her voice delicate. "We're not here to scold you."

My tears threatened to spill. "Kaki, I'm so sorry."

"It's not your fault. If only we knew, we'd never have put you through any of this."

I stole a quick glance at my mother for help. What do I say? How do I respond?

"I want to apologize on Ankit's behalf," Nina Kaki continued, her voice thick with concern.

My heart snapped into two pieces hearing her troubled tone. "No, Kaki. You don't have to."

"Yes, I do," she insisted. Her gaze dropped to her lap. "Ankit shouldn't have treated you the way he did."

I assumed she was referring to the party. How Ankit disrespected me and my people. But what came out of her mouth threw me off guard.

"We knew about Priya," she confessed, her eyes filled with regret. "His friend from the university. They met in London."

A bitter sense of betrayal pierced through my already broken heart. When I was here waiting for his calls and messages, staying up all night shedding tears; he was out there with another girl who probably didn't know the whole truth either.

"He mentioned her a couple of times but only as a friend," she said. "Recently, I suspected something was up. The way he was behaving. All those messages and ignored phone calls. His pale face," her voice trembled, searching for the right words. "We thought it was you he was fighting with. But then, Priya called him a couple of nights ago when he was asleep, so I answered the phone." Guilt laced her tone as she told me the entire story, right from the beginning.

Priya and Ankit went to the same university. They quickly became friends and started dating. They'd spend all day together. While Ankit thought it was all casual, Priya genuinely liked him and fell in love. When she proposed to him, he panicked and flew to India sooner than he had planned. Heartbroken, Priya tried to persuade him. When he didn't budge, she began threatening him.

"You know what he told her?" Nina Kaki sighed, her hand still clasped in mine. "My parents won't agree. They're forcing me to marry my childhood friend."

He was just using me to get rid of her. A dull ache settled within me. How can a person change so much?

"I don't know where I failed to raise him," Nina Kaki whispered.

"Don't say that, Nina," my mother soothed. "You did everything you could. Kids make mistakes. I'm sure he'll realize that."

A bitter chuckle escaped Vikram Kaka's throat, booming into the living room. "Careless, that's what he is," he muttered, rubbing his forehead in frustration. He leaned forward, arms resting on his knees. "Nupur beti, we're a family and we will remain one despite my son's stupidity. So please don't distance yourself from us. I know it's too much to ask for after what he did."

"Vikram Kaka," I managed a steady voice. "I would never do that."

He nodded. "Thank you. We're truly sorry."

Nina Kaki sniffled. "How much we wanted you as our daughter-in-law."

I wiped her tears with my scarf. "Kaki, am I not already your daughter?"

A warm smile spread across her face at last. She pulled me closer. "Of course, you are. But I was so looking forward to bringing you home. We never thought Ankit would hurt your feelings. I don't know how much to apologize."

"You don't have to, Kaki" I assured her, returning her embrace.

As the initial shock of the conversation faded away, Nina Kaki freely spoke to me. They were, in fact, upset with me at first. Like any parents, they simply trusted their son's narrative over my father's explanation. Later, Vikram Kaka profusely apologized to my father. Ankit though, never bothered apologizing to anyone. His ego is too big to even accept his mistake. But I'm not concerned. He'll come to his senses, hopefully. I was more concerned about Nina Kaki and Vikram Kaka. And Priya? I hope she's okay.

The tension in the room began to ease as the dinnertime approached. I persuaded Nina Kaki and Vikram Kaka to stay for dinner. Aai and I prepared a quick comfort food-Dal, Rice, Roti, and Aloo Gobi. We all gathered around the dining table. The awkwardness between Baba and Vikram Kaka slowly dissolved over a meal. Though we all were a little on the edge, the conversation flowed smoothly between us.

After dinner, Nina Kaki pulled me aside. She was holding a small blue velvet box in her hand.

"What is it, Kaki?" I asked.

"This is for you," she said, her voice soft.

I opened it to find gorgeous pearl earrings. "Kaki, I can't accept these. These are yours."

She smiled. "I always wanted you to have them."

"But, Kaki..."

"I don't have a daughter of my own. You're my only daughter, Nupur. And look," she said, holding the earrings to my ears. "They suit you."

I reluctantly accepted the earrings, pulling Nina Kaki into a hug. She cupped my face in her palms and kissed my forehead. "I hope you find someone who'll love you and care for you the way you deserve, my child." A tiny teardrop landed on my arm. I thought it was Nina Kaki's. But it was mine. Nina Kaki wiped my tears with her soft hands. "God bless you," she said, before leaving.

Later that night, as I lay on my bed replaying the events of the day, my parents peeked into my room. Sitting up, I scooted over to make space for them.

"You okay?" Aai asked.

I nodded, resting my head on her shoulder. "I am. But Aai, Nina Kaki, she gave me her earrings."

"I know," she smiled, patting my cheek. "It's okay. Wear them next time we see her."

Baba ruffled my hair playfully. "Sleep early today. We have to go get those chairs tomorrow."

My parents stayed for a bit longer, ensuring I was alright. Finally, after a long time, I truly felt okay. The truth had been revealed, freeing me from the torture. Ankit's behavior still stung me. But I'm not expecting anything from him anymore. Not even an apology. He won't mean it anyway.

Alone in my room much later in the night, my thoughts drifted to Nishant. The image of his worried face as he dropped me off flashed in my mind. He had held my hand throughout the drive home. I couldn't ignore the sudden urge to hear his voice. Reaching for my phone, I dialed his number.

"Hey," he answered breathlessly. "How did it go?"

"Better than expected," I confessed, surprised by the lightness in my voice. I briefly told him about the conversation I had with Ankit's parents.

He sighed, "Wow. I can't believe he did that. You sure you're okay?"

"I am," I assured him. "I really am."

"Ok good. I was getting restless waiting for your call."

I hugged my pillow, tucking the phone under my ear. "I wanna see you."

"Now?"

"Um hm."

"Okay. I'll be on my way in two minutes."

I sat up, chuckling. "No no. I meant video call. Can I?"

"You don't have to ask, Nupur," he said, already switching to video call.

Suddenly flustered, I quickly ran my fingers through my hair and answered the call.

"Hey, beautiful," he greeted me with a smile so captivating, I forgot how to respond.

"How do you look like that in the middle of the night?" I said after a moment.

He chuckled.

"No seriously. I've never seen you in wild hair. Look at me, I'm a mess."

He rolled his eyes. "You're never a mess." He ruffled his own hair. "Better?"

I grinned. "Still handsome."

TWENTY-FOUR

"On the count of three," Vihaan announced, gripping one corner of the new, slightly bigger display case I got for a fantastic discount that I'm still proud of.

Nishant and Baba, each took hold of the remaining corners. With a grunt on Vihaan's cue, they heaved up the case, navigating it carefully into the shop.

"Where do you want it, Nupur?" Vihaan called over his shoulder, a bead of sweat forming on his forehead.

"Right here," I pointed at the spot marked on the carpet, next to the counter.

The men lowered the case onto the carpet and straightened up. "Alright, what's next?" Vihaan asked, wiping his brow.

"That's it for the heavy lifting," I assured them with a grateful smile. "I can handle the rest from here."

Nishant stole a quick glance at my father and then at me. "We could spare another hour if you need any help."

"In that case, boys," Baba said, pointing at the shelves kept by the empty wall. "Help me fix those shelves and then we're mostly done."

While the men effortlessly secured the shelves to the walls, I busied myself with arranging the tables and chairs both inside and on the newly refurbished patio. The once-empty colorless shop, now painted in soothing pastel pink and white resembled a shop out of my fairytale.

Perched on a stool, I took a moment to appreciate the transformation of the shop over the past couple of weeks. It took more days than I had anticipated, but I decided to trust the process. Last night I decorated the empty spaces on the walls with art stickers. The 'Memory wall' adorned with cherished photographs complimented the gift shelves and the card rack. A glorious new coffee machine stood proudly on the counter, waiting to brew fresh coffee for customers. The menu card with a matching design and a range of new items was kept on each table.

It was all so surreal. A dream I had poured my heart and soul into, finally taking shape. The uncertainty hanging above my head long disappeared. If I hadn't lost my previous shop, I wouldn't have been able to create something more beautiful so soon. As they say, everything happens for a reason.

"All finished?" Vihaan asked, dusting his hands.

"Yes, and thank you so much for taking the time to help out. You've all been lifesavers."

"No need to thank us," Vihaan said. "Hope you didn't forget about doughnuts?"

I laughed and gestured towards a box kept on the counter. "All yours."

Vihaan grinned. "Cool, thanks!"

"It's delicious," Nishant smiled at me for a brief moment before looking away, a bit intimidated by my father's presence.

A knowing smile played on my lips. My father isn't particularly saying anything to him. But I can't blame Nishant. I'd be equally nervous when I meet his parents tomorrow. I've invited them to the opening ceremony and I'm already freaking out.

Tomorrow is an important day for me. Not only because I'm reopening my shop, but I've invited an important guest without whom the day won't be complete. I've posted an invitation on my social media channels for my customers to visit the new location and try out the new menu.

It's exciting and a little bit scary too.

"I'm heading home for a while," Baba declared, wiping his face with a napkin.

"Sure, Baba," I replied, rising from the stool and walking over to him. "Go take a well-deserved nap."

He smiled. "Right then. My holiday is over. Back to work tomorrow, I suppose." The truth is, he is more excited about the reopening than I am. He's looking forward to returning to his usual spot behind the counter and ringing up orders. He's even ironed his clothes and set a pair aside for tomorrow. He's adorable.

"Thank you again, boys," he shook hands with Vihaan and offered an extra-firm handshake to Nishant. "Appreciate your help."

I chuckled under my breath. My parents were happy when I told them about Nishant. Aai adores him. Baba likes him too, but he's not showing it yet. 'He's a sensible boy,' he said. 'But I'll be keeping an eye on him. Gotta make sure he isn't troubling my daughter. Can't make the same mistake again.' Baba still hasn't recovered from what Ankit did.

"Anytime, sir," Nishant responded with an equally firm handshake.

As soon as Baba left, Nishant sighed and whispered, "Your father is scary."

I burst into laughter. "Don't worry. You'll be friends soon."

Suddenly, happy chatter of two girls poured into the shop. "Are those doughnuts?" Rutu chirped. With a paper bag clutched in her hand, she skipped directly to the box of doughnuts, followed by Avni who paused to admire the interior with delight. "Everything looks amazing, Nupur."

"Couldn't have done it without you guys."

Rutu finished the last bite of a doughnut by licking her fingers and gave me the paper bag. "This is for you."

"Thanks." I fiddled inside. Out came lacy white tablecloths and curtains, custom-made to match my shop's decor. Rutu recently made matching pieces for Avni's café too, and when I placed an order, she eagerly began working on it. She handpicked the fabric and lace herself and stopped by the shop to take measurements. "It's gorgeous, Rutu. Thanks a lot."

She rubbed her hands together. "Let's get this done!" She and Avni hung the curtains and spread the tablecloths, their enthusiasm echoing into the shop.

Meanwhile, Nishant and I worked on stringing fairy lights around the shelves and the windows, their soft glow added a touch of charm to the space.

"Hey, Nupur?" Vihaan called. "Mind if I try your new coffee maker?"

I found him already fiddling with the plug. "Not at all. Go ahead," I smiled.

Avni raised her hand, "I'd like some coffee too."

"Me too," Rutu added.

"Coming right up." He plucked coffee mugs from the cabinet above the counter and looked over his shoulder. "So Nishant? I suppose you'll be spending more time here now?"

Avni and Rutu giggled.

I blushed, sneaking a glance at Nishant. "I guess," he replied. "I like it here."

"I'm sure Nupur won't have time for us too," Rutu said, teasingly.

"That's not true, you guys."

Now that they know about us, they never let go of a chance to tease us. Turned out they knew. Nishant had talked to Avni about it. He requested her to keep it a secret from me because of Ankit. They're all so happy that it all worked out.

We spent the next hour enjoying a freshly brewed cup of coffee with some cookies and made final touches to the decor. After setting up all the appliances and filling the containers with ingredients, I sighed in satisfaction, ready to jump on a new journey. Having my friends equally excited about the re-opening tomorrow warmed the center of my heart. Their support throughout the last few weeks had been a constant source of strength.

As my friends began to take their leave, I cleared up our coffee mugs and prepped the kitchenette for tomorrow. Nishant lingered behind, tapping his fingers on the counter.

"What?" I asked.

His arm went behind my waist, pulling me close. I crashed into his chest, momentarily frozen. He brushed my hair aside with a free hand and held my gaze. "I'm so proud of you." He kissed my forehead, then trailed down to kiss my cheek, and left a soft kiss against my neck, making me shiver.

"I won't be able to finish these tasks if you keep distracting me."

"Um hm." he whispered, kissing my earlobe and stepping a little away. Flustered, I turned around to sort the utensils. Nishant wrapped his arms around my belly and kissed the top of my head.

I met his gaze over my shoulder. "Your parents and Prachiti are coming tomorrow, right?"

"They won't miss it for anything. Prachiti is so excited, she already picked an outfit for all of us and she was browsing Amazon for a long time, trying to find a perfect gift for the shopwarming."

"She's a sweetheart," I smiled, sorting the piping nozzles in a drawer.

I turned around to face him again. He trapped me by resting his hands on the counter on either side of me. Leaning closer, he brushed a feather-soft kiss on my lips. I instinctively gripped his shirt and closed my eyes. He grazed my nose with his and pulled back, a smile lingering on his lips.

"Baba?" I gasped, looking at the kitchenette door. Nishant snapped away from me so quickly, I was surprised he didn't sprain his ankle. Eyes wide, he dared a glance at the door and glared at me. I burst out laughing, running away from him.

"Why'd you do that to my poor heart?" he ran behind me, catching me in his arms. In one swift moment, he turned me towards him and held me close against his chest.

"Sorry, I was just teasing," I melted into his arms.

"I almost had a heart attack."

I pressed my hand to feel his heartbeat. "Wow. You truly were scared."

"That's not because of your little prank," he mumbled, looking into my eyes.

"Then?"

"It's you," he said. "You make my heart race every damn day, Nupur."

I rose on my toes, held his cheeks in my hands, and kissed him, my very own fairy tale unfolding before me.

Baking Magic

Where every treat comes with a sprinkle of love.

Cakes

Butterscotch	300
Vanilla	300
Black Forest	320
Kitkat Cake	320
Oreo Cake	320
Pineapple	340
Blueberry	340
Red Velvet	350
Irish Coffee	350
Chocolate Temptation	400
Belgian Chocolate Cake	500
Cheesecake	600
(Blueberry/Chocolate/Pineapple)	

Cookies

Butter Cookies 250 grams	110
Choco Chip 250 grams	150
Ginger Lime 250 grams	150

Coffee

Espresso Shot	50
Cappuccino	80
Cold Coffee	60

Cupcakes

Vanilla	70
Coffee	70
Fruit	75
Choco Chip	85
Blueberry	85

Doughnuts

Classic Glazed	75
Rainbow Sprinkles	80
Chocolate	100
Mocha	100

Croissants

Classic Butter	120
Vanilla Cream	130
Chocolate	150

Custom Cakes

Celebrate with our custom cakes! We take orders for birthdays, weddings, and other events. Contact us.

TWENTY-FIVE

I hummed along to a song playing on my portable speaker in my new kitchenette as I iced the cake, rediscovering that familiar sense of comfort in baking. The stress of the weeks leading up to this evening faded away as I traced delicate patterns on the cake and placed it among the rest of the treats in a display case that looked so colorful and vibrant, my heart rejoiced.

The usual sweet scent lingered around me, soothing my ever-growing nervousness for the re-opening. I hung my apron to the hook and took a moment to blend into this new life of mine. Everything seemed so different now, yet nothing changed at all. I'm still the same Nupur, baking cakes and cookies. My shop is bigger now, and so are my dreams.

I walked up to the door and flipped the sign to *Open*. This very moment seemed so out of reach a month ago. I replaced all those nights when I doubted my capabilities with the days that brought me here.

"All set?" Baba asked from his usual position behind the counter, with a flash of excitement in his eyes. He looked sharp in his freshly ironed shirt and trousers.

"Yes, Baba. All set," I replied with a smile.

Aai, looking radiant in her silk saree, carefully placed the Ganesha murti from my old shop on its designated platform next to the billing counter. Taking Ganpati Bappa's and my parent's blessing filled me with a surge of confidence. I was ready to embark on this new journey.

Guests will arrive any moment now. Apart from the entire Rhythm Lane, I was expecting my regular customers who had sent me best wishes along with a promise to pay a visit, and a few food vloggers who had graciously accepted my Instagram collab invitation.

Aai brushed her feather-soft fingers on my cheeks. "Your Baba and I are so proud of you."

I wrapped my hand around her shoulder. "Thanks, Aai."

My parents are happy. What more does a girl want? Their excitement has been through the roof ever since Girija Kaki agreed to lease out her shop to me, which reminded me that she was supposed to be here by now.

"I'll go check if Girija Kaki is ready," I said.

The back door creaked as Girija Kaki entered, adjusting the pallu of her saree. "Sorry, I'm late." She approached us with a bright smile, carrying a cardboard box. "This is for you, Nupur beti," she eagerly beamed. "Come on, open it."

"What's in it?" I asked, intrigued. Carefully tearing the tape, I opened the box revealing six ceramic plates, each with a different print of cupcakes and cookies. I beamed at her, delighted to know she remembered. "You made these? I love all of them."

Her face glowed with pride. "Just a little something for the grand opening. I only had time for six, but I can always make more if you need them."

"These are perfect, Kaki. Thank you so much. But I said I'll buy them from you. Let me know how much I owe you?"

She chuckled, waving a dismissive hand. "It's a gift."

"Thank you so much, Kaki. I'll put them to good use today," I promised, arranging the plates on the shelf.

Soon enough, guests began pouring in. Chaturvedi Ajji and Ajoba were the first to arrive followed by Avni, Vihaan, Amrita Kaki, Tanvi Vahini, and little Nidhi. I saw Rutu rushing through the gates of her hostel next door. She stumbled inside, claiming a seat at Avni's table.

I sprang to action, serving coffee with cookies and croissants. Chaturvedi Ajji was quite curious about the new menu. She requested to try doughnuts and her whole face lit up when she ate one. "Well, this is interesting," she pulled my cheeks. "Well done with the new place, beti."

"Thank you, Ajji." I took her and Ajoba's blessings and carried on welcoming my customers.

At half past six, Nishant walked in, looking all handsome, flashing a charming smile at me. His sister and parents followed him in. Prachiti stepped forward and smiled, "Congratulations, Nupur Di! I got you this."

I opened her gift to find an adorable business card holder shaped like a dough mixer.

"Oh wow. I love it. Thank you."

She beamed and hugged me. Ever since Nishant and I told her about us, she's over the moon. 'I knew it,' she'd squealed. 'The way Dada looked at you, so obvious.'

As Prachiti freed me and floated to Avni's table, I shifted my focus to Mr. and Mrs. Raut.

"Hello Suniti Kaki, Sanjay Kaka." My nervous greetings to his parents earned me a chuckle from Nishant.

"Nupur *beti*," Suniti Kaki affectionately lifted my chin. "Nice shop. Congratulations!" She gave me a beautiful bouquet of pink and white roses.

"These flowers are gorgeous, Kaki. Thank you. I'll put them in a vase. Please take a seat," I ushered them in. Aai and Baba rushed to greet them, directing them to the table reserved just for them. Our parents fell into a friendly conversation so quickly. Nishant and I didn't even have to introduce them.

"Would you like some coffee?" I asked, already on my way to the coffee machine.

"I'd love some," Suniti Kaki replied. "And those cookies look amazing. Maybe some muffins...you know you sent those blueberry muffins with Nishant the other day? Do you happen to have those?"

"Absolutely, Kaki. I heard you liked them so I made extra for you to take home."

She beamed. "You're a sweetheart."

"I'll be right back, Kaki."

Filling a vase with water, I placed the flowers on the counter. Watching our parents getting along so well touched my heart. I stole a glance at Nishant and found him already looking at me. He winked at me and I had to look away to hide my flushed cheeks.

As I brewed fresh coffee and offered muffins and pastries around the room, the gentle murmur of chatter filled the air, blending in with the soft music playing in the background. People complimented the decor, savored the treats, and refilled their coffee cups. I snapped pictures of the moment I'd been waiting for so long.

"It's going really well, isn't it?" Aai said, her eyes sparkling. "All the guests are here."

I smiled at her. "A couple of more special guests are on the way."

"Who?" she asked, keeping the dirty plates beneath the counter and pulling out the clean ones.

"You'll see," I replied.

She shuffled a little closer to me and whispered, "I like them. Nishant's parents. Good people."

"I'm glad to see you all bonding."

"I've invited them home after this, for dinner," Aai told me.

"I think that's a great idea."

She nodded. "So I'll probably leave early to prepare dinner."

"No problem, Aai. But wait for an hour. I have something planned."

I glanced at my watch and then at the door. *Any moment now.*

"Who's coming?" Aai asked.

The bell over the door chimed, and in walked a young woman followed by her boyfriend and her father.

"They're here, Aai."

"Sanika!" A gasp escaped Girija Kaki's lips. Her eyes widened in shock. "Avdhut?" Her trembling voice drew everyone's attention.

Aai's jaw dropped. "How did you manage to invite them?" she whispered. I only smiled.

The three of them made their way to Girija Kaki's table. She stood up, still in shock to see her daughter and husband standing before her.

Sanika wrapped her mother in an embrace. "Aai. How are you?"

Girija Kaki's eyes watered. She looked between them, unable to say a word. "I'm well," she managed to reply. "When did you all come? Why didn't you call?" Questions stumbled out of her lips.

"It was Nupur's idea to surprise you," Sanika nodded towards me.

Girija Kaki's eyes flicked to me. She wiped her tears and smiled.

Avdhut Kaka stepped forward, a hesitant smile lingered on his face. "How are you, Girija?"

"I'm okay," she sniffled. "How are you?"

"Better," he said. He looked at his daughter and the young man standing behind her. "Sanika? Aren't you going to introduce us?"

"Oh, yes. Sorry," Sanika stepped aside to usher her boyfriend forward. "Aai, baba, this is Rahul. Rahul, these are my parents."

"Hi," his tone and posture mimicked Sanika's nervousness. "Nice to meet you all."

Girija Kaki smiled at him. "Hello, *beta*. I'm glad you're here."

Avdhut Kaka patted his back. "Nice to meet you, Rahul. Stay with us for a few days so we can all get to know each other."

"I'd like that," Rahul replied once he got a nod from Sanika.

Avdhut Kaka looked at his wife and smiled. "We heard you're opening a shop, Girija?"

"It's Nupur's shop," Girija Kaki corrected. "I'm only here to support."

"Actually," I decided to step in at that moment. "Girija Kaki, if you could join me for a moment?"

"What's going on?" She asked, glancing at her daughter. Sanika gently nudged her forward. "It's okay, Aai. Go on."

Her gaze drifted towards me standing by a shelf hidden behind a curtain. It was quite a task keeping it a secret. But with Rutu and Avni's help, I managed. Those two were the only people who knew about the surprise.

When Sanika encouraged her, Girija Kaki made her way to my side. All curious eyes shifted to us.

"Everyone," I addressed the guests. "Thank you all for joining me today on this special occasion. *Baking Magic* is incomplete without your support and best wishes."

My parents watched me from the side, eagerly waiting for the curtain to be drawn.

"It's not just my cake shop. It's equally yours. And it's Girija Kaki's too." I turned to her. "Kaki, please do the honors."

She was still unsure when she pulled the string, revealing a shelf filled with a few ceramic pots, bowls, and vases that I managed to sneak in.

"Kaki, you always wanted to start your own business. You can run your workshop from the back room and sell your craft here in our gifts section. It's all yours. This is your shop too," I said, squeezing her hand.

"But this...how did you manage this?"

"I had to sneak in some of your work here," I bit my tongue.

"Aai," Sanika perked up. "I know you wanted to start this shop with me. But I've got a job that I love. That doesn't mean you shouldn't follow your dreams. Nupur is here for you. We're all here for you."

"Yes, Kaki," I added. "You helped me when I needed it the most. This is the least I can do."

"I don't know what to say," Kaki whispered, curiously examining the shelf.

"Say yes, Aai," Sanika excitedly urged. "You can finally live your dream."

A hush fell over the shop as everyone waited for Kaki's answer. The silence stretched for a moment, and then a joyous sob escaped Kaki's lips.

"Thank you, Nupur!" she exclaimed, her face lighting up. "Yes, I'll do it!"

I turned to the guests. "Everyone, Baking Magic is officially resuming business and from now on, the gifts section will be managed by Girija Sawant."

Cheers erupted in the shop as my parents began to clap. Girija Kaki's eyes sparkled with renewed purpose and determination. She pulled me into a hug, promising to fill the gift shelf with more and more creations. Some of the neighbors and customers already purchased ceramic vases to support Girija Kaki.

By the end of the evening, most of the display case and gift shelf were empty. The vloggers I had invited recorded a bunch of videos, snapped pictures, and generously promoted my cake shop. My best friends, my neighbors, and my family showered me with blessings.

And as I took in my surroundings, I knew that this was just the beginning of a new chapter.

TWENTY-SIX
EPILOGUE

Nishant

"Come on!" I called over my shoulder, stalling my bicycle by the slope that goes towards the hill. "We don't wanna miss the sunrise."

Nupur, seated in the middle of the road with her cycle parked aside huffed and shook her head. "I can't," she yelled, rubbing her legs. "Come get me. I don't want to torture my legs anymore."

She looked adorable in her oversized fluffy pink hoodie, sweatpants, and shoes. Her hair was tangled in a claw clip.

"You can do it," I said, my voice echoing around us. "Drink some water and get up here."

She reached for a bottle of water hooked to the cycle, took a sip, and rose to her feet with a much dramatic sigh. "Here I come," she said, slowly riding up to join me. She paused by my side and leaned over to rest her cheek against my shoulder. "Next time, we'll just drive here, okay?"

I laughed. "Okay."

A few nights ago, when I asked her if she'd like to ride a bicycle and watch the sunrise with me from the hills behind CVR College, she nodded with determination. "Yes. Let's do it this Sunday."

And when I asked her if she was comfortable riding a bicycle up the hill, she furrowed her eyebrows. "What do you mean? Of course, I'm comfortable riding a bicycle."

"Do you want to go on a motorcycle ride instead?"

She was only more offended. "No. In fact. I'll race you up the hill."

"You sure?" I'd teased and she'd made a face at me.

We had an early morning date I was so looking forward to. I got permission from her parents to let me take her home for dinner and spend the night with my family, so we could get up early to reach the hill in time. My mother made Paneer tikka Biryani with gravy and raita that Nupur so thoroughly enjoyed. "Kaki, you've to teach me how to make this."

"Only if you teach me how to bake such a spongy cake," my mother replied.

"Deal," Nupur said, shaking hands with my mother.

My father gave Nupur a tour of our house and shared a lot of embarrassing stories of my childhood. Nupur giggled and asked questions to prompt more stories that my father was more than happy to share.

And Prachiti? She was thrilled to have Nupur share her room for the night. They painted their nails, traded earrings, and discussed shampoos, moisturizers, and whatnot. I know too much about tinted lip balms now than ever.

She was shy at first, a little too anxious to spend time with my family. But as soon as she entered my house she switched into her chatty mode. Prachiti's presence made her feel comfortable. Watching her effortlessly blend into my family made me so happy, I couldn't believe my luck.

I've never been in love before. I dated a girl in college for about three months. She was nice but she wasn't the love of my life. We went on a couple of movie dates but it was pretty much a good friendship. Not a relationship. We didn't even break up. We just drifted apart. After that, no girl took my breath away until I met Nupur.

I can never forget that moment when she smiled at me for the first time. I was confused the whole day. I walked around with this urge to see her again, to make her smile, to hear those infectious giggles. That girl entered my mind, my heart, and never left.

It was getting difficult to see her every day and not tell her how I felt. But then I found out about Ankit and everything changed. No, I wasn't heartbroken. I decided to be her good friend. I'm still furious at Ankit for breaking her precious heart, for making her cry. My heart never ached as much as it did when I saw tears in her eyes.

I want to be the reason behind her smile. She looks happy in her new shop. She's taking more event orders and helping Girija Kaki sell ceramic crafts. She also managed to reunite Girija Kaki's family and bring her husband back. Girija Kaki isn't alone anymore and I'm so proud of Nupur for doing that. Now I spend pretty much every evening in her shop, quietly working aside, only jumping to help if she asks for it.

I'm getting used to her presence in my life. Her lavender scent. The fragrance of her shampoo in her hair. The way she walks beside me holding my hand. The way she grips my shirt every time she hugs me, buries her face in the crook of my neck, and leaves small kisses. I'd be lost without her.

"What happened to racing me up to the hill?" I asked, rubbing her back.

She smiled sheepishly. "That was a bit much commitment, I guess."

"You guess?"

She shoved at my shoulder. "Don't be mean. I'm hungry already," she whined.

"We're eating breakfast after this. I'm taking you to my favorite place. You'll love it."

She nodded. "Can't wait."

"Here's a tip," I said, getting ready to ride ahead. "If you don't talk at all until we reach, you'll save some energy."

She rolled her eyes. "Fine!"

To my surprise, she was quiet until we parked our cycles next to a tree and walked the rest of the way up to find a nice spot to sit. Nupur spread a rug, took off her shoes, and slumped to the floor. I sat down next to her, wrapping my arm around her.

"It's so peaceful up here," she said, leaning into me.

"It is," I replied, planting a soft kiss on her forehead. The morning air was cold but comforting. Birds chirped around us. Tree leaves whistled along the breeze.

"When was the last time you came here?" she asked, gazing at the green hills waiting to be bathed in sunshine.

"A few months ago. I used to come here with my friends, but nobody has that kind of time now. So I come here alone, mostly after a stressful week. It calms me down."

She turned to look at me. "Thanks for bringing me here. I love it."

"I love you," I whispered.

"I love you, too," she kissed my cheek and smiled at me as the first ray of sunshine painted a golden glow on the horizon. Green hills illuminated, welcoming us to greet the sun.

Slowly, the sun began its arrival from behind the hills. Nupur's whole face lit up. Her smile widened. "That's beautiful," she murmured, lacing her fingers into mine.

As she witnessed the sunrise, I watched her, the sunshine in my life. She looked so at peace I couldn't take my eyes away from her. I've watched enough sunrises, but nothing as beautiful.

She scooted closer and rested her head on my shoulder and I felt like the luckiest guy in the world.

ᑭᑭᑭ

Enjoyed visiting Baking Magic? Support my indie author journey by leaving a rating and review on <u>Amazon</u> and <u>Goodreads</u>. It would mean the world to me.

Say Hi to me on Social Media: @ruchapantoji

About Rucha

Rucha Pantoji is a self-published author and a content writer. She started writing stories when she was in school, dreaming about publishing her books. But as she grew up, destiny brought her into an Engineering College and she briefly pretended to have her life together by taking a (pretty boring) tech job.

After hating her job and complaining about it every damn day, she finally decided to write stories rather than lines of code. Now she spends her day writing and night curled up in a bed with her Kindle until her eyes burn. Brewing a refreshing Chai is her hobby apart from collecting cute stationery and handbags.

Note from the Author

Dear Reader,

Thanks a lot for reading 'Sweet as a Cupcake'. If any of the incidents put a smile on your face, I'd be beyond happy.

I tried my best to avoid typos. However, sometimes, mistakes do slip through unintentionally. If you find any mistakes, please email me at ruchaaa8@gmail.com or message me on Instagram.

I always like to connect with readers and fellow writers. Feel free to contact me if you have anything to share with me. I would love to know what you are working on.

Once again, thank you for reading my book :)